Praise for THE WEST

"Variously fantastic, comic, elegiac and nostalgic, Mr. Stack's fiction is versatile and engaging...a vivid, compassionate, authentic voice... securing (him) a place in the celebrated tradition of his country's storytelling."

— *New York Times Book Review*

"There's a genuinely wild and fugitive comic sense in these tales that puts one in mind of Myles na Gopaleen as much as the salt spume dam, George Makay Brown. Never sentimental, often funny, always accurate, this is pithy, finely tuned writing of a high order."

— *The Observer*

"Eddie Stack would drive you mad with merriment. He would also make you sigh soulfully for the human condition...Put away the Jennifer Johnston, the William Trevor, the Molly Keane...and take up this little volume of delights."

— *Irish Edition*

"Exceptionally fine tuned...an authentic voice of the migrant Irish."

— *San Francisco Chronicle*

"Haunting stories...filled with beautifully sketched characters. A lively storyteller in a long and hallowed tradition."

— *Philadelphia Inquirer*

The West

Stories from Ireland

EDDIE STACK

TINTAUN

First published in the United States by Island House, 1989

First published in the United Kingdom by Bloomsbury, 1990

This paperback edition published by Tintaun, 2010

ISBN 978-1-930579-07-1

TINTAUN MEDIA
Galway & San Francisco

Do mo mhúintir

(For my people)

"Time Passes" was first read on KPFA Radio, Berkeley, California, and was later published in *The Irishman*, San Francisco

"For the Record" originally appeared in *Criterion 83*

"Limbo" appears in *Modern Fiction about School Teaching: An Anthology*

"The Warrior Carty" appears in *The Clare Anthology*

"Time Passes," "Limbo," "Revolution" and "The Warrior Carty" are read by Eddie Stack on "Stories from Ireland,"a spoken word recording with music by Martin Hayes and Dennis Cahill.

See www.eddiestack.com for more information.

THE COVER IMAGE

The cover image is 'Blake's Corner,' a painting by Phillip Morrison, a North Clare artist. Built in the eighteenth century, the two shops, Blake's and Linnane's, are some of the oldest buildings in Ennistymon, County Clare, where many of the stories in this book are set. They are classic examples of vernacular architecture with their colourful shop fronts and Moher flag roofs, and are Protected Structures. Both stand below road level and have stone steps leading down to the entrances. Blake's was a small bar and confectionary shop where I bought penny sweets on my way to school. Linnane's was a hardware store for tradesmen and farmers.

'Blake's Corner' and many images of Clare landscapes, streetscapes and people are available from www.phillipmorrison.com

~ *The Stories* ~

Time Passes   9

For the Record   17

Limbo   33

Bláth na Spéire   45

Revolution   75

The Warrior Carty   83

Derramore   95

Time Passes

We often threatened to take the Boat on those wintery mornings after Christmas, while we waited for the dole office to open. Huddled in deep doorways, sheltering from the spray blown up from the river, we shook our heads in despair. We were sentenced to another year's penance in the wind and rain. Another year in a world of shuttered shops.

There would be no market until the Saturday before Saint Patrick's Day and it was common knowledge that some shopkeepers – bored and bothered by the stillness – would take to their beds for weeks at a time, only surfacing for the funerals that always followed the rain. There would be people in town for the funerals. The funerals, the Mass and the dole brought us together to complain and spend the government's money on cold porter. And the more we drank, the more pitiful our situation seemed, grown men being paid by the government to remain on the census sheets and being despised for doing so.

But yet we stayed. For some obscure patriotic reason we lingered on in that place where there was neither hope of work nor lover. We passed the year threatening to leave for England and retelling tales we heard from the Lads. There was another world on the far side of the water and the Lads were in the thick of it. They were our heroes in those days.

9

Altar boys who went to Camden Town wearing scapulars and came home with blue tattoos. Seven days a week they worked in the midst of rogues and ruffians, ripping up roads and pouring concrete so they could spend Christmas in Ireland.

They arrived the evening before Christmas Eve on a special train that brought them from the Mail Boat, and from early afternoon that seldom-seen station was the liveliest place in town. Stalls sold hot soup and toffee apples and two women from Barranna hawked naggons of poteen for half the price of shop whiskey. The school choir sang carols and Father White collected money for a new church from a dwindling congregation. For the first time in almost a year, laughter and song drowned the sound of the roaring brown river and months of gloom vanished like the night.

Hours before the train was due, groups of young people walked up and down the windswept platform, cajoling with railway officials and shouting false alarms. The more anxious preferred to wait in the colder waiting room, or sit on icy grey platform benches. Cloaked in scarves and shawls, country women crunched clove sweets because they were too shy to smoke in public. Their husbands sucked pipes and looked up and down the rusty track, conferred with railway officials and reported home.

By four o'clock the gas lanterns were lit and hackney drivers arrived, muffled in coats and scarves. These shrewd men noted what parties were in attendance, what fares to expect, who to solicit and who to avoid. They only left their warm cars when excitement peaked and everyone swarmed to the platform, peering up the line and listening to the harassed rumblings of the approaching Steamer.

The Lads emerged from the dimly lit carriages to a rousing reception of cheers, waves and back slaps. Pink faced and closely shaven they looked angelic. Helpers and hackney drivers took their brown bulging suitcases and Father White's choir sang "Come All Ye Faithful." We all joined in. Parents shyly welcomed home their young with tears and we sang louder and marched around the platform. Gloria, Gloria, it was really Christmas.

But there was always someone or other who failed to return, even through they had written to say they were coming. Bewildered relatives put a brave face on grief.

"They might arrive for the New Year," they said.

We nodded in agreement, even though we knew better.

The Lads passed their first night at home and were brought up to date with the year's happenings, the weather, the state of the country, church collections and other burdens the plain people had to bear. Old and new news was exchanged until the travellers showed signs of fatigue. Then they were urged to go to bed with a glass of hot punch and a sprinkle of Knock water.

On Christmas Eve they came to town with their parents and drank moderately in long-ago haunts while the old people did the shopping and attended confessions. There was no end to their money on that day, loans were offered freely and drinks were bought for everyone who wished them well, enquired about the sea crossing or asked:

"How're things across the Pond?"

And things beyond were always good.

11

By Saint Stephen's Day all family dues and duties had been attended to and the Lads rambled to town after breakfast, packing the small bars and attracting hoards of hangers on. It was a day of banging doors, thirsty Paddies criss-crossing town in shoals of blue suits. Bars steamed with sweat, smoke and after-shave lotion. Floors were littered with charred Swan matches, Senior Service cigarette ends and bronze thrupenny bits, left for late night sweepers. Pubs hummed every time the Queen's face decorated the counter – no monarch had ever raised so many smiles in Ireland.

And later when the Wrenboys descended on the town with flute, fiddle and tambourine, we jumped for joy. We had the best of all worlds then – the Queen's money and plenty music, in our own backyard.

As time passed, old acquaintances were renewed and the Lads trusted us with tales about the parish's forgotten sons and daughters. These secrets were imparted in the strictest confidence and later retold with the same sentiments. Every second year Rufus Ryan, a man who had emigrated long before I was born, had another wife. Jim Flynn was either in or out of jail. One year we heard in detail why Pat Browne left the priesthood and took up the shovel. And why Mary Scully went on the game after a tempestuous marriage to a Welshman. Hatchet O'Day met her in a boarding house and she cried in his arms and begged him not to tell. But he did, and more.

The Lads began to wither as more time was spent in the pubs than at home. By the fifth day of Christmas, the blue suits were creased and crumpled, white shirts were stout stained and London socks left unchanged. In the mornings, eyes were bloodshot and watery and the Lads resorted to drinking hot whiskey to line their stomachs. They were in topping form by the time faithful friends and professional listeners arrived.

Their stories and antics brought Kilburn closer to us. We quickly became familiar with the "Tube" and knew the stops on the Circle Line, the Picadilly and the Jubilee. We heard about their haunts and habits. Wild sprees in Camden Town and dicey nights in the Galtymore. Saturday sessions in the White Hart, Quirke Road Church for Sunday's Irish papers.

Each year we discovered anew that there was little comparison between life at home and in London. The Lads pointed out that we had few comforts. No Soho. Or no Chinese caffs where waiters bowed and took your coat. And bowed again when they served you unidentifiable piles of food, at four shillings for two. We often had to sympathize with them for bothering to return home at all, and they always looked us in the eye and said, "If it weren't for d'aul lad and d'aul lady, I don't think I'd bother."

And yet they spent little of their holiday at home. They preferred instead to entertain us with stories about subbies from Roscommon, granite hard gangers from Connemara and sly foremen from Cork. All tough men who were respected for their crookedness and cruelty to others.

As the days trickled away our heroes became slovenly, sometimes unruly, often drunk. The sessions were lengthy and sometimes in the evenings, a brother or sister might be dispatched to town in an effort to coax them home for dinner. But they preferred to linger on in the smoke-filled bars and chew dry turkey sandwiches at the counter, turning around between mouthfuls to quip, "You'll never go back, scobie."

They regularly fell asleep beside pub fires, waking unexpectedly to startle us with songs from London jukeboxes. Some got awkward when they were refused more drink: publicans were insulted, glasses were broken.

The last day or two of their holiday was spent at home with their families, and on the Sixth of January they left again for London. Lonesome men with empty pockets and brave faces, seen off from the station by weeping women and stone eyed old men. There were no hackney cars, no helpers, no stalls, no hymns. The green train rolled into the rain and stole Christmas with it.

Ivy and holly were taken from the walls, the Crib and decorations were stored away for another year and there was a hush in the countryside. We heard the wind and the river again and felt the grey drabness of January that paved the days for Lent. It was a lonely period when even clocks refused to pass the time and their hands lingered between hours for hours on end, or so it seemed. Again we threatened to take the Boat, lonely for company and the spirit that had been whisked away from us. Weeks passed before we got into step with the year and then Christmas became a legend, one to be compared with previous ones.

But time passes, and when Christmas came around again the Lads dutifully returned home. They came every year until the government closed down the railway line, shuttered the station and sold the track to small farmers. Dublin turned its back on us and London slipped further and further away. Then the journey home became full of obstacles and hazards.

After a few Christmases the Lads gave up the ghost. When they did come home it was for family funerals, and then they drank too much and cried too much. Angry tears for stolen years. In drink-stained whispers they promised to come home the following Christmas, for old time's sake.

But we rarely saw them again. There was nothing left to return to and the Lads moved on. Life had set its course and school friends drifted away without warning. Time tricked us and it became too late to change, too late to take the Boat, too late to wake up.

We are still on the census sheets and still drinking pints of cold porter for the government when we meet for the dole, the Mass and the funerals. But there is little life in the public houses, now colder than the station waiting room. Only postmortems are held here in these ghost-ridden rooms where jackdaws block smokeless chimneys. And yet they are our only refuge. It is here we are forced to shelter before moving through the Winter.

Time passes, but memories linger.

For the Record

Wild and windswept, the hill of Clontom rose like Alcatraz from a sea of black, bubbling bogs. Often shrouded in blankets of rain, drizzle or fog, the peak spent half its life in heaven. From its high rocky slopes, numerous springs and streams weaved their way through the gorse-covered granite and down to the bogs. One summer, they sparkled so brilliantly in the sunshine that nine families were lured to Clontom. Goaded by folktales, they hopelessly panned for gold. But the land was cruel and without compassion. Over time, one by one the families departed for greener pastures, until Clontom tolerated only one household, the 'Dawler' Moores.

Tommo and Dommo Moore were in their late fifties and their spinster sister Megga was a little older. A younger sister called Dodo was forced to emigrate to America many years previously when cheated in love by a blacksmith's son. Like the generations before them, the Moores had little stock: a few sinewy geese, three bantam hens, a cross cock and a couple of bedraggled goats, who provided more company than sustenance. Once they kept a wild white cow, but hunger forced her to stray down the mountain and across the hazardous bog, honeycombed with deep dank pools. Her saunter came to grief when she tried to wade through a bottomless drain.

This was the first bit of commotion in the region since the gold rush and the loss brought the Moores closer together in the same way a family death sometimes might. Megga said the mishap was a sign to forsake agriculture and return to the old family trade of poteen making. The brothers agreed and since that fateful day, they used the climate, isolation and crystal clear streams to their advantage, and developed a thriving distilling business. Their poteen was noted for its punch and purity, a reputation which guaranteed its popularity and an ever-growing market.

Tommo made the moonshine and took enormous pride in his craft. He was considered a master distiller by many authorities and fussed and cared, tested and tasted the wash regularly, to ensure its high quality. After each run he thanked and praised God for sending the rain.

"Tis all in the water," he used say humbly.

Whatever the weather or season, Tommo never ceased to be happy and when not distilling, he fished the streams and drains for eels and small speckled trout. Unlike his brother, he wore neither cap nor hat but bared his bald, bulb-shaped head to the elements. Tommo always dressed in black clerical clothes which Father Gill (a customer and holy man from a distant parish) consigned to him every Christmas. Like his sister, he was tall and overweight but they had little else in common.

Megga was the outrider. Every month she lumbered down the narrow, steep and slippery mountain track and carefully picked her way through the treacherous bog. She travelled for days on a shaky bicycle, burdened with bags of clinking bottles. She called on the buyers here and there and returned with the money, provisions and the mail from Dodo, which she collected at the post office.

Megga was a stern woman who never displayed signs of emotion, though thoughts of company-keeping seldom let her be. She confided this in Father Gill and he told her to trust in God. Ever after when he bought poteen, he gave her religious magazines which Dommo would read aloud at nighttime.

Dommo was the brainy brother. On Dommo rested the responsibilities of maintaining the still, the bicycle and the wooden churn, as well as all forms of reading and writing. Sometimes Dodo mailed him back issues of *Popular Mechanics* and other technical journals which he delighted in reading. He would study the magazines for days before relating articles and inventions to the others while they sat around the smouldering fire at night-time, drinking unwracked poteen. Dommo considered himself smarter than the others but kept his feelings private.

One evening Megga chuckled homewards with a large well-wrapped parcel and a letter, both from Dodo, as well as the usual provisions. She laid two heavy canvas shopping bags on the table, gave Dommo the letter and retreated to her bedroom with the parcel. Tommo rooted through the provisions and described the items to his brother, who nodded while he read Dodo's long letter.

"Twelve bottles of stout...what's this?...Jam, two crocks of red jam. A piece of green bacon...tay and sugar...snuff and tabaccy...and Great God Almighty...three new clay pipes. The poor cratur has a heart of gold. Flour, a stone of brown flour...a new enamel mug..."

Megga emerged from her room and coughed loudly, the brothers turned and stared at her in deadpan disbelief. She walked around the kitchen once or twice before soliciting their opinions on her new clothes. Tommo was first to find words.

"Oh, but they are beautiful, beautiful...only pure beautiful. And the lovely colors, beautiful blue, a color that suits you Megga. And so unusual, very unusual cut...what is it called?"

"Dommo, what does she call it in the letter?" she asked.

"Hold on...hold on 'till I see...I'm sendin' Megga a sailor's suit I bought at a sale in Macy's. A sailor's suit, that's what she called it..."

Megga beamed and purred as she stroked the striped sleeve of her tunic. She took a seat by the fire and related the news from beyond the bogs. Her brothers were quiet but she was full of life.

"An' that's all the news I have for ye now," she said eventually. "Tommo, open a few bottles o' porter like a good lad. Had Dodo any news, Dommo?"

The candle was lit, the snuff and porter was passed around and Dommo read aloud the letter from Dodo. The emigrant wrote of many things. Tex Guinan was gone to California and Marcus Doyle had lost another boxing match. She conveyed good wishes to long-departed neighbors and relatives, advised Megga on how to clean the suit and concluded her letter with a mention of a craze that was sweeping America. Dance bands. She wrote:

"They are very good and earn big wages. The men play all sorts of strange instruments and many of them smile a lot. All the bands have singers and a good few of them are women, all the men go mad for the lady singers and some of them are married a few times. But of all the singers I have heard, I don't think any of them could come near Megga, she had such a lovely voice. I often think of her and cry. I remember how well she sang thirty years ago. If she was here, she would easily make a position with a big band and earn a lot of money, she might even meet a husband or some sort of a man."

"She's awful good and always thinks of you, Megga," said Tommo.

"God love her, the cratur, and she thinks there's still neighbors around here."

They stared at the fire and silently thought about poor Dodo. She was a gentle soul and Tommo remembered her as a slight young girl with a pale face and wiry curling red hair, a pious girl. Dommo recalled how she made butter for the market and saved her money for a dowry from an early age. Megga remembered how she was jilted in love by a youth with a squint and left home disillusioned and brokenhearted. She hung a black iron pot over the fire and broke the silence.

"How long is she gone, tis never thirty years."

"Oh God, tis, and a lot more," confirmed Tommo, opening three more bottles of porter.

"I remember it well," reminisced Dommo. "Twas out in the year. Shure she wrote after landin'. I remember it well. It took her six days to get to Queenstown and twenty more to reach America."

"Tis awful far," sighed Megga, thinking about the dance bands and the dancers, "awful far entirely."

Again they drank in silence, and when the pot began to bubble, Tommo fetched three enamel mugs and made large portions of sweet, hot poteen. He said with a tremor of nostalgia in his voice, "Do you know, Megga, we didn't hear you singin' for ages."

"Well now, that's right," agreed Dommo, "an awful long time indeed. How well Dodo remembers your voice, and of course, you had great songs, too."

"The very best, and she could sing them too, great songs and auld wans as well," reminded Tommo.

"Like 'The Old Bog Road,' and the other wan..."

"Lovely Lissnashee," said Megga, eyes misting and heart swelling.

"The very wan, wan of your best and an awful auld wan, that's right. 'Lovely Lissnashee,'" exclaimed Tommo.

"Awful auld, shure," agreed Megga, "and the kind that the Yanks would love to hear."

She poked the fire and added more turf. She saw visions of tall, dark, sincere men dance with the flickering flames, and without warning she burst into song. Tommo bolted upright and Dommo froze with his knees crossed uncomfortably. Her voice was coarse, rusty and forced and she wandered aimlessly in and out of various keys. 'Lovely Lissnashee' was a song of exultation but Megga reduced it to a plaintive dirge. Tommo encouraged her as she strove to reach some high notes, but her voice turned shrill and suddenly plummeted almost an octave. When she finished the song, Megga felt haggard and harrowed. She realized that age was creeping upon her. But she held a brave face and there and then instructed Dommo to write and tell Dodo how well she could sing down all those years.

After that night she became a compulsive warbler and sang on every possible occasion. She sang war songs and wrong songs, love songs and sad songs. Day and night she droned and moaned in a most searing and provoking voice. There was little peace in Clontom until she took to the roads again with a bicycle load of poteen.

Megga tarried in the low lands longer that usual but this did not alarm the brothers. Though neither of them said it, they relished the lull. Dommo took pen and paper to crags higher up the hill and wrote some poetry: odes to the snipe, curlew and lapwing. Tommo strolled across the marshy ground and thought about the bygone days and nights, when nine families eked a living from Clontom's unfruitful soil. He got lost in a mist of memories.

They were grading poteen one evening when Megga returned. Immediately Dommo observed that she had a lot of drink taken and knew her moods were fickle. As usual, he received the letter, Tommo scrutinized the provisions and Megga related the news from the lowlands while warming her weather-beaten legs to the fire. When the candle was lit, Dommo read the letter. Dodo informed them that she was changing her employment and asked as usual for their prayers. Then she described her future boss in a fashion that smacked of romance.

"He is a very nice man and his mother came from Swinford in Mayo. Two autos he owns and a great apartment in the better part of Manhattan. He smiles often when I tell him about Clontom but he is happy here..."

Another page was devoted to a social gathering in the Bronx. She wrote how the dance band charmed and wooed the party. How Nan Magee fell in love with the piano player and later tumbled down the stairs after him, using a champagne glass as a parachute. Megga pricked her ears:

"And that band have a record for sale in the shops here. Of course nowadays everyone has a record player or gramophone, they are very handy and sound great. If poor Megga got the chance to make a record she would be famous and make a lot of money..."

Visions of dance bands and crowded ballrooms clouded the singer's eyes. Glasses of champagne clinked in her ears. Sincere men with neatly groomed moustaches held their slender hands towards her, they all had autos, just like Dodo's new boss.

"Lord save us, but if you were in America, Megga, you'd be worth a fortune, God love you," said Tommo. Dommo nodded in agreement.

In appreciation she attempted 'Peter and the Preacher,' a difficult but humorous ditty which strained her capabilities.

Tommo made a round of hot poteen and they discussed dance bands and records. Dommo recalled having read about the gramophone in some technical journals and he was encouraged to search for the articles. He sieved through countless tomes, extracting a volume from the collection every now and again. He returned to the fireside with a batch of books and gave an elaborate account on gramophones, phonographs and nickelodeons, illustrating his lecture with photographs and drawings. Megga studied a close-up photograph of a record for a few minutes and her heart fluttered. She had seen such things for sale in Fogarty's shop, she remembered Father Gill buying one.

Dommo talked for hours and Tommo made too many mugs of punch. Megga attempted to sing on a number of occasions but drink had taken its toll. The brothers carried her to bed and she wept her way to sleep, haunted by nice men in the Bronx who bowed and saluted, while they danced on her greasy goose-feathered pillow. Her night was restless and agitated.

Early in the morning the cold breeze from the bog chilled her back to reality when it whistled through the broken bedroom window. Sluggishly she arose and retrieved from a jug in the kitchen dresser the small leather purse which contained her long-collected dowry. She pinned the purse to her underclothes, sprinkled holy water on herself and headed downhill towards the tar road.

Her sudden departure worried the men, especially when they found her empty dowry jug on the table. For days they conjectured and pondered on their plight. Dommo promised to flatter her singing if she ever returned and Tommo pledged to serve her less potent punch.

"But what'll we do if she comes home with a husband?" he asked.

"What can we do but hope he's someone we know?" said Dommo.

Megga returned just before twilight one wild evening. She was alone and her welcome was heart-warming and without interrogation. She left a neatly-wrapped slim package on the table and sat by the smoking fire. Tommo fussed over his sister and made her a mug of strong tea.

"What's in the aul packet?" he asked.

"A gramophone record."

"My God!" exclaimed Dommo, rushing to the table, "And where did you get it?"

"I bought it in a shop. Where else?" said Megga.

"'It'd be a great change, no doubt, if we had something to play it on, like the machines I see in the books," said Dommo.

"A great change from what?" she challenged. "If you're that smart why don't you make a player? With all your brains and auld books, you should be able to manage something simple like that. I saw wan of them below in Fader Jack Gill's house."

"And how is poor Fader Gill?" asked Tommo.

"Great form altogether, a very brainy man...and a nice man."

Dommo huddled beside the fire and moped. He drank insensibly and theorized about gramophones and records. A few hours later, his speech was slurred when he spoke.

"Do...do ye know what I read in wan of the books while you were gone, Megga? I read...read how they make records in America...1978's they call them."

Megga ignored him but he continued.

"They're simple to make...the 1978's...wance you have what they call...the disc."

"The disc! By gor but learnin' is a great gift," remarked his brother.

"A great gift...and a gift to be shared, Tommo," reminded Megga.

"But anyways…'tis aiser to make or to…to record a gramophone record than 'tis to make a gramophone."

Megga poked the fire and heaped more turf under the black pot. Dark handsome young men darted from the yellow ashes.

"Much aisier altogether shure," she said. "That's what Fader Gill told me. Tommo, top up Dommo's mug like a good fella."

"Could you do the job yourself?" asked Tommo.

"Of course he could. Shure, that fella could make a watch for you. He has brains to burn, brains to burn, didn't I often tell you that, shure."

Dommo got carried away as praise was buttered on him.

"Well…well I s'pose I could come up with some sorta machine that could do the job," he said.

"Of course you could, and it wouldn't be half your best."

"And then Megga could make a record. Maybe we could send it to Dodo and she could sell it. We might get a lot a money. Well, Megga would get a lot a money," said Tommo, clapping his hands like a child.

Next morning, Dommo began researching recording equipment and techniques. He pored over books and manuals that Dodo had sent him, jotting down facts and figures, making countless cross checks and references. His study lasted all day and all night. For the next twelve days it was often dawn before he retired to bed, his oval head revolving in a cushion of theory. But on the thirteenth day, Megga and Tommo arose to find him snoring by the fireplace, a sheaf of papers scattered at his feet. He was gently carried to bed and covered with blankets and old coats.

"The job is done," he said sleepily.

Megga nosed over the worksheets and tried to fathom the formulae and calculations. But her heart thumped when she saw Dommo's drawing of the recording apparatus. Carefully she ran her chubby forefinger over the sketch, looking at it from different angles before asking Tommo for his opinion.

"Well...tis awful simple...well, not simple...but well thought out. Anyway 'tis very good."

Megga frowned and carefully put the papers in the dresser.

"I don't know," she said, "maybe tis too simple."

Dommo slept late into the evening and that night he explained the design and clarified their queries with so much ease and authority that all Megga's doubts and fears were dispelled.

"A marvelous machine and so well thought out. God bless your little head."

"When will you have it made, Dommo?" asked his brother.

"Well, I'll have to go to town for a few bits an' pieces before I can start puttin' it together," he explained, "I was thinkin' of hittin' away in the morn for 'em."

"The sooner the better," Megga said, counting the handsome young men who danced with the flames of the fire.

When he reached town, Dommo set about buying pieces for the recorder. He bought a roll of strong wire and a roll of thin, thread-like wire in Mungovan's. Tommy Vaughan sold him a packet of strong darning needles, nuts and bolts, a small hacksaw and a collection of assorted metal clips. He went to Coco Ryan the blacksmith with a few sketches and ordered various shapes of iron plate.

"It'll take a few days to get this forged," figured Coco, so Dommo adjourned to McFadden's Bar, where for three rainy days and nights he drank and sported with urban sages he had not seen for six or seven years. He heard strange tales about Megga's singing at weddings and wakes, and serious stories of visiting missionaries denouncing poteen and house dancing. They wondered about his visit to town but he assured them nothing was amiss. He was making a more efficient still that would increase their production and steady the price of poteen. They admired his principles and toasted his health.

When he returned home, Dommo set about constructing the machine immediately. Tommo watched him admiringly, clay pipe dangling, eager to lend assistance. First, a sturdy frame was erected and firmly fixed to a huge flagstone in the center of the yard. On this he mounted the bicycle, making certain the wheels could clear the ground and rotate without obstruction. He checked the chain tension and inspected the pedals. Meanwhile, Tommo located the butter churn and greased all the moving parts. This they positioned beside the bicycle, confirmed the drum could rotate at a steady pace and then adjourned to the house for the most delicate part of the operation.

Dommo placed Megga's record on the table and threaded a long steel bolt through the centroid of the disc. His brother and sister watched silently. Dommo measured distances, referred to his calculations and when satisfied, fastened the bolt in position. Megga sighed with relief and Tommo smiled.

The bolted record was brought to the yard and fixed to the back axle of the bicycle so it revolved with the wheel. To the saddle neck Dommo attached Coco Ryan's fabricated metal arm which held a darning needle at the tip. Carefully he placed the needle in the outer groove of the disc, ordered Tommo to hold it in place until he adjusted springs and clips. Megga viewed the technicians with confidence and romanticised about the Bronx and tall dark men with big motor cars. Soon she would meet them, dressed in her sailor suit. It would be good-bye to Clontom for good and glory, good riddance to Father Gill's advice and the rickety bike.

She was called to the yard about four o'clock that evening. Dommo placed a timber box near the churn and motioned her to sit on it. Measurements were checked for the last time, the churn moved a shade and the drum tilted until it was the correct distance from her head. Finally a thin wire was secured to the drum of the churn and attached to the record needle. Dommo issued last minute instructions and mounted the bicycle. He pedaled at a steady rate and the record hummed.

"Now!" shouted the cyclist and Tommo wound the churn rhythmically.

The brothers looked anxiously at Megga. She cleared her throat but her lips remained sealed. Her jaws rattled and teeth chattered. Before her eyes fame and fortune whirled inside the raging churn. Thousands of faceless men waved and blew kisses to her but she remained mute, sweating in despair and embarrassment.

"Megga!" roared Tommo, causing her to shriek into verse.

"Lovely Lissnashee...what a fine place to beeee...with grand companieee...Brandiee flowin'...an' fellas blowin'..."

As the song progressed, her confidence strengthened and Megga embellished the piece with yodels and intonations, ending it with a lingering yelp. Tommo congratulated her.

"Well fair play ta yeh Megga, aul stock! You never lost it. Twas yer best yet. The very best."

"Yerra I don't know, I think I took it a bit too high."

"What high? Not at all. Twas beautiful, pure lovely," he assured, linking her to the shelter of the kitchen.

Dommo dismantled the apparatus and took the disc to the house. Carefully he peeled the label from the record and replaced it with one that read "Lovely Lissnashee sung by Megga Moore, Clontom, Ireland."

"We'll bring it down to Fader Gill in the morn and he'll play it for us," he announced.

It was evening when they reached the parochial house and Father Gill was pleased, if puzzled to see them. He was a robust man, middle-aged with a balding head and permanently bloodshot eyes. A pleasant man, never without his black leather bound breviary or a word of advice for his flock. He ushered the Moores into the parlour and asked his housekeeper to bring tea and scones.

"God bless you, Fader," thanked Tommo, accepting a cigarette from the priest.

"We came to ask you a little favour, Fader," began Dommo.

The priest nodded, glancing at Megga's sailor suit. Dommo continued,

"Well, you see Fader, tis like this...you see Megga made a gramophone record..."

"I recorded wan, Fader," corrected Megga, "and we were wonderin' if you could play it for us before we send it to Dodo."

"Ah yes, poor Dodo," reflected the priest, "what a grand surprise it will be for her and she beyond in America, ah yes. Of course I'll play it for ye. What song did you sing, Megga?"

"Lovely Lissnashee."

"Ah, great heavens, my favorite ballad."

"That's right Fader," beamed Megga.

"Only a very fine singer can sing that song. Your mother, God be good to her, made a great job of it. Where's the record?"

Dommo unwrapped the disc and handed it to the clergyman, who examined the hand-printed label.

"Lovely Lissnashee..." he muttered curiously.

The gramophone sat on a round mahogany table by the window. Gently, Father Gill placed the record on the turntable and cranked the handle. Dommo watched with interest and Tommo winked at Megga. The priest carefully lowered the arm and the great timber horn cackled to life. The parlour filled with the husky voice of a female singer accompanied by a ragtime pianist. The Moores stared at the gramophone, recognizing neither singer nor song. When it finished, Father Gill enquired if they might like to hear the recording again. They shook their heads in silence.

"Well, I'm sure Dodo will be delighted with it," he said. "An unusual rendition of the song, and one I have not heard before. Your own interpretation no doubt...but tell me, who is playing the piano?"

"Dommo, Fader," muttered Megga as she watched hundreds of handsome dark men wave good-bye and disappear into the twilight outside.

"Ah yes, poor Dommo," smiled Father Gill.

Limbo

Sounds from the town seeped through the tall Monastery windows and mingled with the Hail Mary. The whine of the sawmill, milk churns rattling home from the creamery. Horse carts creaking. Motor cars honking, people hailing each other. An assurance that there was another world out there after school. Some day, the Monastery would only be a memory. But now we were having a prayer break with Brother Mahon.

Back at class he resumes the tirade, prancing around the room like Groucho Marx. Mahoney hears the little rattle as he passes and writes PILLS on the cover of his grammar book. I make a check mark with my finger: Brother was back on the pills alright, it was written all over the Monastery.

"The trouble with ye is that ye don't want to learn," he fumed. "Now it isn't the lack of brains that's affectin' ye...and I'm sayin' that in plain English so that ye'll understand me...no...ye have brains alright... but ye're as lazy as Sin."

He halted behind the table and waved a bundle of homework copies like a tomahawk. He glared at us and asked, "Have ye any shame?"

Then he closed his eyes and leaned forward on his tiptoes. A smile ran around the class.

"Alright," he whispered, dropping the bundle of blue copy books on the table with a dull thud.

"Alright. Now a simple three-page composition called 'What I Can See from My Front Door' is not a lot to ask twenty hardy young fifteen-year-old fellows to do...I was making it easy for ye."

He paused and his eyes shot open.

"But such...such utter trash," he wailed, "such utter filth...I have never read in my entire life. Stop grinning Horan! I'll wipe that leer off your puss when your turn comes, and you can be sure of that my boy!"

Brother Mahon could go any way with the pills. Sometimes he jumped over desks three at a time, kicked our school bags and glared at us like he said God would on the Last Day. Other times he could be great fun and tell us stories about the world and how happy he was to be a monk. One day he played the tin whistle in class and we sang rebel songs, but that only happened once. It was hard to tell how the dice might roll with the pills. But things were looking grey today. Today he had no hope for us. He said we had nothing to look forward to but *an Bád Bán*: the emigration boat. We were born to emigrate, he said it was in our blood. We were not worth educating, sons of small farmers and publicans, we were the flotsam left behind by the tide. His eyes closed slowly and he beckoned us to stand. Another Hail Mary for Our Lady smiling in the corner.

Brother Mahon rapped the copies against the table.

"I have a few right gems here. First, O'Loughlin's. Where is O'Loughlin?"

"Here brother."

"O'Loughlin, what in Hell's Blue Blazes are you doing sitting in Friel's desk?"

"Brother O'Brien put me here."

"Am I Brother O'Brien? Am I? Is this Brother O'Brien's class? Come up here near me! And stay in your own sty in future!"

O'Loughlin moved like a defendant crossing the courtroom.

"Now," began Brother Mahon, "we all know that Master O'Loughlin is descended from a great line of bards. His family were once Chief Bards to the Earl of Killty...but that was a long time ago. Now O'Loughlin... tell us where you live."

"Castletown brother."

"Louder."

"CASTLETOWN."

"Now O'Loughlin, if you live in Castletown, how in the name of God and his Blessed Mother can you see the Aran Islands from your front door? And before you answer, spell Island?"

"O-i-l-a-n-d."

"Dooney. Spell Island for your cousin."

"I-s-l-a-n-d."

"Now O'Loughlin. Remember that, you glugger head. But now, tell us how you can see Aran from your front door."

"I was just using my imagination," he muttered.

"Well don't bother to use your imagination, use your brains instead. Sit down and give me peace."

He made exceptions for O'Loughlin, who had an uncle in Brother Mahon's order. O'Loughlin was timid. But not so his cousin, Dooney.

"Dooney did you write this?"

"I did brother."

"Are you sure you didn't get a bit of help from someone."

"No brother – I mean yes brother."

"Which is it?"

"I did it myself brother."

"Hand me up a copy without paw marks the next time."

Coyne was nibbling paper when his turn came.

"Coyne, you fathead!" bellowed the monk. "Stop chewing the cud like a good bullock."

Coyne was a nervous wreck and fidgeted with the piece of paper he had been nibbling. A white envelope with a note from his mother which he handed to the monk.

"What is it this time?" he mocked, "Ye ran out of candles? Or have you given me that excuse already?"

Brother Mahon knew that Dada Coyne drank the creamery check every month and was more often in court than most lawyers. Willie could only muster up a half page about a view that was part of a nightmare. Brother Mahon read the note, closed his eyes and whispered, "Take this copy back and have a full page for me by Friday."

He beckoned us to rise for another prayer.

A few copies skimmed through the air, nothing of great substance, fair attempts conceded the monk. Then there was Murphy's. Waving Murphy's copy, he glanced around the room. Murphy had switched seats and was now sitting at Clancy's desk.

"Murphy! Yes you! Get back to your own stable. What in the name of God are you doing in Clancy's seat?"

He didn't answer, just flashed a grin and zipped back to his own perch. Murphy was world-wise, smoked Woodbines, drank beer, backed horses and played poker. For him, school was a place to pass adolescence, punch in time between summers and getting wiser in the ways of the outside world. He had run away from three boarding schools before joining our team, a high-risk pupil, even though he was the sergeant's son. He had the finest of vistas from his front door, his house looked down on the town and the strand. But he ignored it all and wrote about the Monastery instead. Brother Mahon cleared his throat and read in a mocking voice:

"*The Monastery was built in 1829 by a band of monks from Dublin. It has very big gardens and one time the monks used to make cider which they sold. The monastery is across the road from the dance hall...*"

He shook his head.

"I was waiting for him to tell me that the band of monks played in the dance hall. Trash! Murphy, what in the name of God has any of this tripe to do with anything?"

Murphy shrugged and smiled as if saying 'life's like that.' A nervous titter escaped from the back bench and Kerrigan was ordered to stand at the head of the room and face the statue of Our Lady.

"It's the likes of you, Kerrigan, who encourage Murphy to dish up this tripe. And I wouldn't mind, but nowhere does he mention the name of the monastery. Murphy, stand up! What is the name of this school?"

"Saint...ahmm...the Monastery."

The monk looked at us and shook his head.

"Saint Patrick's!" he howled, arching his back like a cat. "But what does it matter to you? Your father'll find your way into some job. Sit down you clown."

Malone's copy fell apart as it sailed over our heads, cover departing from body. Mine was next, then Friel's, then Horan's.

"Horan, come up here to me. Do you hear me? Come up!"

Horan edged to the head of the room and the monk withdrew the black leather cosh from his robe.

"Out with it," he ordered.

Horan's hand trembled and the monk lashed it six times, becoming more demonic with every stroke. His eyes were blazing and his head and neck glowed when he turned around.

"Horan," he panted, "handed me up a yarn about a football match. It had nothing to do with his front door, he titled it 'A day I will always remember.'"

The taste of blood put Brother Mahon into another world. The animal in him was roused and he became a schoolboy's nightmare. His nostrils flared and he looked possessed, satanic. The voice got shriller and he strutted around the room pelting abuse at us. We were failures, and if we were the best our parents could produce, then God help Ireland. But while we were in class we would pay attention to him and do the correct homework, not like Horan.

He rummaged through the copies. He was frantic, and scattered them all over the table until he pulled Kerrigan's from the chaos.

"Where are you Kerrigan?"

"Behind you brother."

"Well stand over here where we can see you...and don't always be looking like a moon calf. Kerrigan? What is the meaning of this drivel? Where do you live?"

"Boland's Lane."

"Boland's Lane what?"

"Boland's Lane, brother."

"Alright. And have you anything else to write about but a...a tinkers' brawl? Hah? How dare you hand me up this...this drivel about two families of tinkers murdering each other!"

"That's all I could think of...we had Yanks home from Boston..."

"Shut up you lout and come here to me!"

Brother Mahon gaffed him by the ear and lifted him like a piece of meat. Kerrigan pleaded, "Brother, brother..."

"Now listen to this all of ye. Kerrigan is the type of fool who is a cute fool. When he leaves here in a couple of years what will he do? Like his father before him, his first port of call will be the dole office. Then he'll put his feet up, warm his toes to the fire and wait for Wednesday, dole day. Alright...he'll get married, get a council house, free milk and shoes. His wife will give him a child every year and when they're crying for attention, our hero will be down the town, strapping pints of porter or holding up Coleman's Corner with his broad back, passing smart remarks to other cute fools like himself. Alright?"

Kerrigan wept and wriggled. He staggered loose with a yelp and jumped away from Brother Mahon.

"Go back to your hovel, Kerrigan."

The class was battered, beaten and humiliated. The monk closed his eyes slowly and whispered that we could always pray. Prayer could move mountains and even get us to heaven, if we were lucky. But we were too lazy to pray, he said distantly. And everything began with prayer. If we didn't pray right, then nothing could be right.

From there he wandered off to the foreign missions and explained the great work monks were doing harvesting souls in darkest Africa. He wondered aloud if any of us would like to take up the work. But our heroes were not in the black cloth. Anyway, seams of outside world had already permeated the class. Cigarette smoking was rife, swearing was commonplace and girls came up in conversation. There were no vocations here.

A cloud came over his brow when he picked the last blue copy book from the table. The main feature.

"Stand up, Gregory McNamara, and face the class. Now, McNamara, I know all your brothers and those who went before them, but you are the worst of the brood, you great big jackass. What in the name of God do you mean by handing me up a shovel of dung like this for my breakfast? What?"

His eyes darted from pupil to copy.

"A simple essay that a nine-year old child in the heart of London could write...and a fifteen-year old *sutach* from Ballyglan can only come up with this...this manure."

McNamara was doomed for the back streets of Soho like his brothers before him, Brother Mahon told us. Bound for sleaze and slaughter. Not even a flicker of hope for him.

"Stand to attention McNamara...and face me...and before we start...the next time you hand me up a copy, give me one without the butter and jam...spare the butter and jam for your lunch. Alright? Alright, to begin at the beginning:

'*It was only early yesterday morning that I was wondering what kind of view we would have if we had a front door to our house. We have only a back door to the kitchen...*' Alright? So far, so good...but listen to this...'*Our house faces north...*' Spelled n-o-r-d...'*in the direction of Russia where Napoleon was born...*"

His voice trailed off in horror.

"I'll read that again, just in case ye didn't hear it...'*in the direction of Russia where Napoleon was born.*' And listen to what comes next...'*The great monk Rasputin was Napoleon's son and a neighbor of my grandmother's knew Rasputin.*'"

A red flag to a bull. Brother Mahon was aghast. He closed his eyes and seemed to be praying for patience, or the school bell or maybe a pill.

"That's true," bungled McNamara. "Oh God...my grandmother told me that."

"You bloody bogman!" bellowed Brother Mahon, tears in his eyes. "You Heretic! How dare you insist that Napoleon was born in Russia... or that he sired Rasputin."

McNamara blushed and looked towards the Blessed Virgin. The monk was breathing heavily, his knobbly fists clenched white.

"And on top of all that heresy, McNamara drops this bombshell on me...'*they make great vodka in Russia.*' They make great vodka in Russia! What in the name of God and his Blessed Mother has all or any of this to do with the great view you have from the front door ye don't have? Answer me McNamara, you ass!"

McNamara awkwardly shifted his weight from foot to foot and stared at his desk. Brother Mahon was tortured. Mention of drink, Rasputin and red Russia in the same page was the height of treason. He dabbed the beads of sweat from his brow.

"ANSWER ME!" he screamed, stamping his foot.

"I was stuck for something to say," McNamara said suddenly, hoping to stonewall the charging monk.

Gregory ducked Brother Mahon's fist and slid under the desk like an eel. The monk ordered him to stand by the wall, firing in threats of expulsion and terms in hell. He moved in on his prey and lashed out his boot as McNamara darted beneath the desks. We scattered out of their way and grouped at the head of the class room.

"Jaysuz lads," whispered Murphy, "but this is serious."

"Come out of it McNamara! Out!" roared Brother Mahon, kicking over school bags and thumping desks. "Come out of it and get up to the Superior, you pagan!"

He flushed McNamara from cover and lunged at him with a primeval groan. Suddenly, alarm flashed across Brother Mahon's face. We saw him stagger, then tumble heavily on the floor, brought down by Murphy's schoolbag. The door banged and McNamara was home. The monk was robbed of the kill.

Brother Mahon struggled to his feet and dusted himself. He stared at us, and looked bewildered, as if he had just fallen through the roof.

"What are ye doing standing there like a flock of sheep?" he asked, "Go back to your seats! Quickly!"

We were only sitting down when he ordered us to stand and face the statue of the Blessed Virgin.

"We are now going to offer up a decade of the rosary for those in need," he said quietly, eyes closing slowly.

"In the name of the Father, the Son and the Holy Ghost," began Brother Mahon, tears rolling down his face.

Bláth na Spéire
(Flower of the Sky)

On the second Sunday of every month, regardless of the weather, we gathered in Pat Patrick's cottage to discuss the affairs of the world. It was a safe place. Surrounded by wind-bent bushes and haggard trees, a thatched cottage built against a stone humpbacked bridge that crossed no water and spanned to nowhere. The only place you could go from here was home the way you came.

For centuries this cottage had been the venue for soirees and dances. But now the girls were all married, or gone to America, and only the bachelors came and some men who were married for so long that they never remembered having done so. But they were all fine men and each carried his cross with silent dignity. Ocras Burke named Pat Patrick's cottage 'The Sanctuary.' Like the rest of us, he felt safe there. It was a refuge from a changing world, and though the journey there was weary and unsheltered, it cleansed us like a pilgrimage.

When the government stopped the house dancing, Pat Patrick gave up farming and took to distilling poteen as a form of protest. A simple barter system took care of his needs and he never looked back from that day on. Two ounces of plug tobacco could be exchanged for one bottle, two pounds of tea for the same, pork steak and puddings were worth two bottles and so on. The trading was a secret business, transacted in whispers over a cluttered table in the corner.

When business was finished, Pat Patrick raked up the open fire and crowned it with a pyramid of turf. His nephew Bachus Tobin swept the floor, lowered the oil lamps and attended to the six wag-of-the-wall clocks, silent since our last visit. He painfully wound each of the clocks until they tick-tocked to life, but never set their hands. Like death masks, they stared blankly from the flickering shadows, ticking out of time and chiming out of rhyme, each with its unique flourish. Palem Folan said they made nonsense of time and Uaigneas Gallagher said the cottage was like a huge time bomb. After the clock ritual, Pat Patrick left a large basin on the floor, filled it with poteen while Bachus gave everyone a mug and announced, "There's a drop in the basin if any of ye are thirsty."

The night was forgotten. Clocks were unheeded and matters of faith and pleasure were discussed, interspersed with music, songs, dancing exhibitions, recitations and arguments. From time to time the tub was topped up with more poteen and if the night was flagging, Bachus prolonged it by encouraging someone to relate a story. Like the rest of us, he hated to leave the Sanctuary before daylight.

I remember a story Pat Patrick told one Sunday night during the month of June. There was a big crowd at the Sanctuary the same night, including the five Softwood brothers and the Folan twins. The weather was warm and there had been some discussion on potato blight and corncrakes beforehand. Somehow the train of conversation changed and Uaigneas Gallagher began lamenting about the scarcity of fairies and blaming the motor cars for driving them away.

"Well," comforted Bachus, pouring another gallon into the basin, "it wasn't the aeroplanes anyway Uaigneas, because they have wings of their own."

"They're not gone anywhere," Pat Patrick said.

Two clocks clamored at once and Ocras reset his pocket watch before joining the conversation.

"As sure as there's an eye in an ass," announced the little dancer in the brown suit that someone had sent him from America, "but they are a strange crowd and still around. What about the rumpus below in Barnagweeha last month?"

Pat Patrick nodded.

"That's right," he said. "I only heard about it the other day when a young man called here collecting money for a new church or school. I told him I had nothing to give. I said I never went to school, I didn't believe in money and wasn't in Barnagweeha for thirty years and didn't intend to go there for another thirty. He said he understood. He was a well-mannered young man who might be a saint sometime in the future. I said all I had to give was a drop to warm himself and he took it. Then he told me about what happened below in the town on May Eve."

"Ahmm, Pat...what was his name?" asked Sultan Softwood, intent on getting every detail of the story correct for the retelling.

"It'll come to me again...Art something or other. A lovely boy."

Chairs were drawn closer and mugs were refilled. Bachus smiled like an angel and gave his uncle a cigarette.

"God help us, but I remember the same night well," continued Pat, lighting the cigarette from a burning piece of turf.

"May Eve it was, and as the young man said, it was a restless night everywhere. Even up here twas bad. Just after dark a flock of small birds roosted under the bridge outside, but left again after a while and burrowed in under the thatch of the cottage, that's how bad twas. The craturs were frightened of somethin' an' kept me awake half the night with their twitterin' an titterin', just like the tom tits when the hawk is overhead. But I didn't mind so much because I had a sprig of May Bough tacked to the door before the sun went down. I knew the house was safe."

"Well of course I didn't venture outside the door 'til morn, but when I did...and this is a strange thing for this part of the country...I found a lady's handkerchief beside the bridge and it had the most beautiful smell of perfume. Now! I had no clue in this wide earthly world how it got there, we are so far away from everywhere and no woman has come this way for the last twenty years or more. But this young man knew how it got there and twas he told me about the racket below in Barnagweeha the night before."

Pat Patrick drew us into the night and unfolded the town with every word. The streets were silent and deserted. Nobody lingered at the corners or in doorways for the customary chat after the pubs had closed. Tonight was May Eve, when even the lopsided moon was too anxious to smile and the starry sky was aloof from the land below. On May Eve the spirits stalked in that darkness that separated heaven and earth. No mortal with any sense walked the ground on such a night. Sergeant Malone even skipped his midnight patrol.

"Well of course," said Pat Patrick, "midnight is when They come and visit the world on May Eve. They travel the country to welcome in the summer, bathe in the rivers and oceans to make them swim with fish, and dance on the land to make it green. And of course it's the one night in the year when a spirit can take a mortal as a lover.

"Well, on May Eve anyway, as the young man told me, the spirits from the Ring of Trá gathered outside the town on Halloran's Hill just before midnight. He said there was fifteen of them in it: Elbib the older, seven Elders and seven Youngers. Elbib Trá sure is well known the world over for his fondness of women."

Pat Patrick told how They journeyed towards Barnagweeha on the stroke of twelve. On the way they were joined by The Blind Hare, a harmless furry grey creature with high ears and large white eyes like golf balls. In another time he had been a piper, but he was transformed for stealing tunes from a musician when Ring Law was harsher.

Passing through fields and streams, They chanted behind the wind and scattered their blessings and dreams over the countryside. Requests from believers were noted, advice was whispered down chimneys and warnings were whistled through keyholes. In appreciation for a favour, They left a purse of gold sovereigns on the window sill of a widow's cottage. And at the edge of the town they stopped and listened to Gleo, Ring Historian and Keeper of Records, narrate how Barnagweeha got its name.

Elbib led the Ring into the town, the Blind Hare following cautiously behind. On the steps of a monument in the square, They sat and looked around the slumbering streets. Tonight it was theirs and in recognition, many householders had a sprig of May Bough tacked to their doors.

"There's no May Bough on the barracks door," noted Grá the Elder.

"And Paudie Quack Ryan has none again this year," added Ceo the Elder.

"Whist," said Elbib, "there's a shop open on Church Street."

49

They moved up the street and from the shadows gawked at the white light and steam billowing from Lee Low's Fish and Chip Shop. They heard Seán and Tanya curse and swear at each other, and Elbib dispatched Luas the Younger to find out what was going on. The Lee Lows were newcomers to the town and unaware of the nature of the night. Normally after the pubs closed they did a roaring trade filling the bellies of hungry drinkers with fast food, but tonight there were no takers.

"People still in pubs," insisted Tanya.

Seán shook his head, chain-smoked cheap cigarettes and battered fish, for the sake of peace.

"I told you!" she crowed when Luas flitted into the greasy shop.

His eyes flashed from the pinball games, cigarette machine and jukebox to the foreign couple behind the high counter. Tanya watched him bounce around the shop.

"Yes please! Can I help you?" she called in a stern voice that turned Seán from the fryer. Never had he seen such an odd being, a baby-faced little man with skin wrinkled like leather and a wild head of brass curls. He concluded that a circus was passing through town.

"Yes please!" Tanya repeated, "What can we get you tonight?"

Luas smiled at her but said nothing. She pointed to the house menu on the wall and called out the fare on offer. Luas frowned and rattled off a series of numbers which she conveyed to Seán as, "Vifteen double chip, thuty singul fish and a large salad for the hare."

As if a password was uttered, abruptly the jukebox blasted rock music and Luas danced around the shop. Packs of cigarettes spewed from the vending machine and the pinball machines zinged hysterically. The chip shop shook with commotion and when the Blind Hare sauntered into the shop Tanya screamed, "Cancel the ordo an get them outza here!"

"Too late, the chips are down," muttered Seán.

He drained the fish and wrapped them in newspaper, smothered the chips with salt and vinegar and whirled a tub of salad from an onion, two carrots and a limp head of lettuce. He placed the banquet in a cardboard box, shouted "To go!" and lit another cigarette. As sudden as it began, the commotion stopped and when Seán turned around, the shop was deserted and Tanya and the money box were gone.

In rage, he stormed from the shop he sweated to keep open and rushed up the street to the barracks. By this hour the night had turned cranky, and the stars and moon were blocked out by low rumbling clouds carried from the ends of the earth on a sharp black breeze.

Seán hammered on the barracks door and shattered Sergeant Malone's dream about riding a rocking horse in the dance hall. The lawman bounded to his feet, straightened his tie and peeped through the security eye. At the sight of Lee Low he was relieved but suddenly angry at being fooled to attention.

"My wife gone with the money," babbled the chef.

"Calm yourself," advised Malone, opening his note book. "Start at the beginning."

Seán did.

"Am I hearing you right?" quizzed the sergeant, narrowing his eyes at the distracted husband.

"Yes!" cried Seán. "All I say is true."

"Can't be true," grunted Malone.

"Just because I Hong Kong man with Russian wife you not believe me?"

"Now listen to me, I have a fat file here already on your wife. Remember she's the ballet dancer who defected at Shannon Airport. History repeats itself in this country."

51

As Malone spoke, clouds of smoke belched down the chimney behind him and his face paled when he remembered there was no fire in the grate. He was getting uncomfortable, getting distracted and wishing Lee Low would go home to Hong Kong. The windows rattled violently and wind screamed under the barrack's door, carrying the moans and groans of history to his ears.

"It must have been a terrible racket," said Sultan Softwood.

"Worse than Dunkirk," yawned one of the Folans.

"Much worse sure," said Pat Patrick, "and to make it worser again, a window was broken, by accident of course, because They don't do things like that. And then a dog barked start to bark, out of fear naturally enough, and other dogs replied. And sure, when the Blind Hare heard them he got petrified with fright. More dogs woke up and barked back at the others, tellin' them to shut up and sure the hare bolted and ran for shelter in the churchyard. Well as soon as that Blind Hare cleared the churchyard wall, every crow and jackdaw that roost in them churchyard trees took to the night. The young man told me they twisted and tumbled over the town cawin' and croakin' for all their worth. And the dogs below barkin', barkin', barkin'. He said it was the wildest night in the history of that side of the world and I'd believe him."

A clock chimed gloomily and Mango Softwood asked, "Ahmm... excuse me Pat Patrick..but where was Mrs. Lee Low?"

"It seems she was with Elbib. He had her under some trance or other and she never missed her husband or knew where she was."

"God help us," whispered Ocras Burke, passing around cigarettes.

"And of course when things were getting out of hand," continued Pat Patrick, "twas then the sergeant was sorry he had no May Bough on his door. There was nothin' he could do. But even those that had the

May Bough up were afraid. Families climbed into the wan bed, holy water was sprinkled around in a circle, window blinds and shutters were closed, just in case. And then, on top of everything, didn't the church bells start to ring out, like the bells of a sinkin' ship and every electrical light in the town was quenched. The town was as black as the belly of a coal mine, and just as cold and as damp. That's the truth."

"I heard that," confirmed Ocras Burke, "and that's often the way before They take someone to the Otherside."

"Oh law-cee-mee," wailed Sika Softwood.

"Amen," muttered Bachus.

In the black barracks the telephone rang hysterically and the police radio screamed obscenities. Malone groped for a candle but hit the floor instead when a dustbin lid crashed through the window and rebounded off the four walls of the day room, skimming over their heads like a discus. The wind roared through the broken window and confidential files and documents were strewn onto the street like feathers from a burst pillow. The barracks were under attack by forces unknown and fearing the worst of the worst, Malone crawled around the room on his hands and knees until he found the back door. With Lee Low at his heels, he made his way through the state strawberry patch and safely reached the crooked laneway that wound behind Main Street.

"Well, staying near the sheltered side of the lane they travelled on all fours and who did they meet, but Tanya Lee Low and she lost in a trance!" Pat Patrick slapped his knee and looked at us.

"They were lucky to find her," Sultan muttered.

"Of course when they shook her she came back to life and screamed with fright, the poor cratur."

Pat Patrick told how the trio battled through briars and nettles until they reached the Turf Fire Inn, a public house that kept irregular hours of business. On hearing the lawman's knock, Martin Herod, the landlord, opened the door.

"Martin Herod, Saint and Scholar," pipped Ocras Burke. He was related to Herod and they were alike. Herod was also a man of low stature, but he dignified this handicap with a genial manner, impeccably groomed hair and well-tailored clothes. Like Ocras, he was also a bachelor who lived in hope, though his wandering eyes and heavy bushy eyebrows often betrayed his anxious mind. Candle in hand and keys jangling like a jailer, Herod led the party along the cobwebbed back corridor and into the bar room, which was dimly lit by a few flickering tilly lamps.

Malone first made a mental note of who was on the premises. At the end of the counter, two chubby youths and a slender woman whispered among themselves. The sergeant knew them as Rodeo, a local country and western band who sometimes played in the Turf Fire Inn. At the corner of the bar, with his broad back propped against the lavatory wall, the landlord's brother sat on a high stool. He was a policeman in Boston when not on holidays and Malone recalled his name was Tom.

Martin Herod treated the latecomers to a drink and fortified by the company, Malone took the Lee Lows aside to interrogate them. Tanya refused to answer his questions and the faraway look in her eyes immediately aroused her husband's suspicions. When Malone pressed her to account for her movements, she mocked and challenged him to stop the miscreants who were tearing the town asunder outside.

"You just like KGB," she snarled.

In a sweat, Malone turned away and lodged himself at the bar.

Tom Herod watched him throw back four stiff whiskeys while he drank one.

"Hey skipper," whispered the Boston cop, "What in the heck is happening outside? This ain't the weather, huh? I wouldn't tolerate it on my beat, Jeeze you guys should be armed."

Malone nodded and rambled through two more whiskeys muttering about the patrol car and the special task force. Tom excused himself and returned with a revolver.

"You can keep this skipper," he whispered, slipping the gun into the sergeant's hand. "I've a few more in my room."

Malone thanked him and they drank together, Tom unfastening a shirt button every now and then as his sobriety slipped. Outside, the ground trembled and the night roared, but Malone felt safe in the company of Tom Herod, who related heroic Boston deeds that only policemen understand. Without warning, Tanya Lee Low barged into their company and chided Malone in front of all present.

"He not brave policecop...he afraid to catch tiny little man and bunny rabbit."

Martin Herod warned her to remain quiet. He was anxious at the state of the night and had no May Bough displayed. Though he went to Mass every Sunday and sometimes to Benediction, Martin believed spirits could be walking in and out of his bar day and night without him knowing it. Nervously polishing glasses, staying within earshot of Mrs. Lee Low and keeping his eye on the girl who sang with the band, the barman didn't notice a tall dark haired man approach the bar until he tapped on the counter.

"Holy Christ! Where did you come from? Who let you in?"

"Good night Martin. Taking shelter from the storm."

Elbib Trá spoke softly. He looked familiar to Martin, having taken the form of the Heineken hero in a TV commercial for the lager. Herod stared at him and wondered where he knew him from.

"Could I have a pint of stout please Martin, and have a small toddy yourself."

While filling the pint, the landlord reported the newcomer to the policemen. Neither recognized him, though they agreed he looked familiar. Brazened by whiskey, Malone went to investigate, gun concealed in his trouser pocket. He pushed out his chest and stepped up to the Older, who was paying Martin for his drink. He took stock of Elbib, noticed a small gold earring in his left ear and wondered if he was a tinker, sailor or fiddle player. Malone took a shot in the dark and asked, "Excuse me sir, but by any chance are you in the antique trade?"

Elbib chuckled into his pint.

"I'm sorry officer," he said. "I've nothing to do with antiques. People collect and pay exorbitant prices for such items for pretentious reasons. But as you want to know my business, I'm actually looking for a lover."

"A lover?" repeated the lawman, beckoning for a drink.

"Yes, a lover."

Malone swallowed a huge mouthful of whiskey, coughed and spluttered and shook his head in the dark.

"Well, you have a difficult task ahead of you in this town. Lovers are an elusive breed and I'd rather face reality any day than hook up with a bad one. Do you know what I'm sayin'?"

Elbib nodded sympathetically and Malone gripped his elbow.

"Listen," he whispered, "like antiques, good lovers, the ones with quality and class, are rare and expensive and often very old."

"Too true," agreed Elbib. "And worse of all, they are often in someone else's sitting room."

"Now you're talkin'," muttered Malone. He nodded slowly and returned to his company.

While relating the interview to Tom Herod, he realized tranquility had returned to the town outside. The bells were silent, the crows roosted again and the dogs dreamed about butcher bones. Malone relaxed and felt braver, attributing the metamorphosis to a psychic warning he had given out once he had a revolver in his possession.

"Of course the reason the town was quiet," explained Pat Patrick, "had nothing to do with Malone. Not at all. Twas quiet because all the Youngers, Elders and Blind Hare had followed Elbib into the pub. They were invisible of course, and so nobody but Elbib knew they were there. But anyway...in order to have some music in honor of May Eve, Elbib let the Blind Hare become his old self. Once again he was a blind piper and Luas brought him to the Older."

The piper was tall and gaunt, slightly stooped with worry, and dressed in black threadbare breeches and torn swallow tails. On his head perched a tall top hat, green and mouldy with age and bad weather, and around his waist were strapped his ancient uilleann pipes, which groaned and squawked as he moved. At the sight of the silhouetted musical figure, Martin Herod blessed himself and brought the stranger to the attention of the policemen. They concluded he was a friend of Elbib's and must have been on the premises earlier.

"He was probably in the lavatory all this time," drawled Tom.

Martin scratched his head and sighed.

"Ah Mister Piper!" greeted Elbib, drawing the musician closer to the counter, "what can I get you?"

"You are very kind to me as always," he lisped. "Would it be in order to trouble you for a large brandy and a pint or two of strong porter?"

After serving them, Martin remained within earshot. They clinked glasses and toasted each other's health.

"Drink and be merry for tomorrow we die," saluted Elbib.

"Hare today, gnome tomorrow," said the piper, "So *bhí* it."

"So what?" demanded Tanya Lee Low, who was standing behind him at the counter.

"So *bhí* it," he repeated, "So *bhí* it."

She fiercely slapped his stubbly grey face. Taken by surprise, the blind musician lost his balance and spilled his pint on Elbib's pants. Elbib stared at Tanya and she shook violently, dropped her glass of vodka and melted into a blob before the late night drinkers. In the darkness her husband bent down, lit a match and recoiled in shock.

"She has become a little frog!" he screamed.

"The Lord between us an' all harm," moaned Uaigneas Gallagher.

Malone blessed himself, Tom Herod took a swig from his drink, Martin craned his neck over the counter, and gazed mouth open at the harmless frog croaking her innocence on the dark floor.

"What in the name of Jesus is happening here?" Martin asked the cops, who stared blankly at each other.

Seán picked her up from the floor and displayed her for all to see. The band screamed, the lawmen turned away and Elbib shook his head wearily. Seán carried his frogwife into the lavatory and placed her on the slippery slope of the cavernous white toilet bowl. He patted her horny head and blew an impassive kiss. The chain jangled, pipes gurgled and she who had nagged him night and day was whisked away in a cascade of water and blue bubbles. Much relieved, he returned to the bar and called a round of drinks for the company. Malone made a mental note of the incident and filed it away for future reference.

To steer everyone's attention away from the mystery, Elbib suggested the piper play some Irish music for Tom Herod, the Boston hero.

"Yeah!" agreed Tom, "Piper, come 'ere. Have a drink on me."

The music relaxed the bar. Drink flowed freely and Tom unfastened two shirt buttons. The Elders were drinking solidly and reciting poetry for the consideration of each other. Out of sight, the Youngers darted behind the bar every now and then, returning with bottles of whiskey and brandy. The piper received mild applause for his music, Tom bought him another drink and stuck a fat cigar between his teeth. Suddenly the musician roared, "SILENCE!"

In the hush that followed, Elbib coughed a couple of times, cleared his throat and crooned softly a haunting song that echoed from the four corners of the bar. Luas sprinkled a fistful of *foideen draoí* – a dark green powder – over the smouldering turf in the grate and a silver mist rolled from the fire and covered the floor knee deep. Elbib lulled the mortals into a gentle trance. The Youngers and Elders joined in the song. Some crooned in harmony, others jingled tambourines, triangles and tin bells. Thorn pipes were aired, brass flutes, humming stones and jaws harps, the Spirits often changing from one instrument to another in the course of a bar of music. And while he drank whiskey with one hand, the piper played a soft bass drone with the other. The bar whirled inside the sound like a spinning top. Scents of moss, musk and dew-blessed flowers drifted through the air and the drinkers were reminded of another time, a far away woodland under a smoky blue sky.

They were puzzled by Elbib's song. Nobody had heard it before and yet it was familiar. The lady singer with the country and western band tilted her head like a bird hearing a mating call and though she didn't understand a word of the song, it still made sense to her. While she wondered who the singer was, Sergeant Malone discreetly tapped her arm and asked how her father was. Noticing the lawman had taken her attention, Elbib called Martin Herod.

"Martin...what is the young lady having? Give her a drink from me."

"Arrah, I think she's fine sir...my brother just bought her a drink."

"Well what is she having?"

"Brandy and Babycham."

"Well then get her a brandy and Babycham....and have one yourself."

Reluctantly Martin served the drink, indicating who had ordered it. The lady smiled at Elbib, a long lingering smile that would have lasted longer had Malone not engaged her in conversation about dance halls. Elbib was ruffled and summoned Martin.

"Have you much champagne in stock Martin?"

"Champagne?"

"Yes...the bubbly stuff."

"I have a crate an' a half of it...not much demand for it ...but I keep it in just in case."

"Put a crate on ice if you will...and Martin, what is that young lady's name?"

"Arrah, she sings with the band that plays here on Tuesday nights..."

"I understand. But who is she? What's her name?"

"She's a fine girl...just turned twenty...an only daughter. All the lads are cracked after her..."

"I don't doubt that...but what is her name?"

"Her father comes in an' out now an' again."

Elbib's eyes darted around the bar like a hawk on a spree. He was getting impatient with Martin, who was babbling on.

"The father thinks the sun shines out of her..."

"Blast you Herod!" rasped Elbib, suddenly grabbing the barman by the collar, "It's not a horse you're trying to sell. All I want to know is her name."

"Mary Ellen MacEarl," spluttered Martin.

"MacEarl, as in fish?" asked Elbib, releasing him.

Martin nodded and backed away from the counter. He opened his shirt collar and ventured, "I hear that she is not that...good...around the house. Not a great cook...according to her father."

"Hmm."

"But there's classes for that sort of thing now sir...the marriage training people hold them above in the convent."

"In the convent? Farewell to bacon and cabbage...By the way Martin, could I have a pen please."

"Certainly sir. Here...but sir, bacon an' cabbage is one of the greatest feeds of all time. Bacon an' cabbage, a reek of floury spuds and a quart a buttermilk to wash it down."

Scribbling something on a beer mat, Elbib muttered, "They say mackerel are nice too, Martin."

"The finest sir. Especially early in the season. But there's lots of fish in the sea sir."

"You're full of wisdom Martin. There's lots of fish in the sea, but so few of them are delicacies. Now, could you pass this to Miss MacEarl, like a good lad."

Martin looked at the beer mat and flushed like a turkey cock. He grew uneasy. Who was this stranger who signed his name E.T.?

"Elbib Trá," piped Bachus, uncorking a bottle.

"And Martin shuffled away from him like some poor devil whose ass was stolen," sighed Pat Patrick.

Mary Ellen MacEarl laughed when she read the note. Malone peered over her shoulder at the scribbled beer mat. He shot a look towards Elbib, grabbed the beer mat and waved it at the Older.

"What's this in aid of? Haw?"

He tore the mat into confetti and knocked over a bar stool to emphasize his anger.

Elbib smiled and shrugged.

"What I do with my socks is my business!" roared Malone.

"Up to a point," said Elbib calmly. "But they are government-issued socks and therefore what you do with them is the taxpayer's business."

Malone smouldered, tossed back someone's drink and growled about hippies. Without warning he violently thumped the counter, upsetting glasses and ashtrays.

"Go aisey sergeant...go aisey for God's sake!" pleaded Martin Herod.

But Malone was beyond reason. He plunged his hand into his trousers and retrieved the revolver. Fumbling with the warm gun in his sweating hands, he suddenly turned like an outlaw in Hollywood and faced Elbib. The policeman raised the weapon and prayed as his finger curled tighter around the trigger. The gun boomed. Youngers and Elders huddled under seats. The country and western band screamed and took refuge in the toilet. But Elbib stood his ground and said, "For God's sake, leave down that toy."

Tom Herod shouted at Malone, and Seán Lee Low grappled with him. Martin lurked under the counter and the gun boomed again, shattering a mirror behind the bar.

After muttering through a decade of the rosary, Martin Herod left his shelter and peeked over the counter. Malone and Lee Low were sprawled on the floor.

"Are they dead?" he whimpered.

"Jus' out for the count, Martin," drawled Tom Herod.

He had seen strange carry-ons in Boston and readily accepted anything he didn't understand. He unfastened another shirt button and stared at Elbib, who frowned and blew smoke rings.

"Tragic," sighed the Older.

"Tragic or magic...they're down," added Tom. "Hey Martin, give us another shot."

Martin looked at him.

"Fill 'em up again."

Martin trembled behind the counter. He worried that there was some sort of conspiracy against him. Unexplainable things happening before his eyes and yet he could not refuse anyone a drink. The world was closing in on him and nobody cared.

"Don't worry," drawled Tom, "be happy Martin. Do you mind if I sing a song?"

Jesus Christ, he wants to sing! thought Martin. We have nothing to sing about.

Tom's song was a sad one called 'My Little Brown Collie.' A train of tragedies, and as it progressed, streams of emotional sweat dribbled down his cheeks. The band returned from the toilet and stepped over Malone and Lee Low as Tom wobbled dangerously on a high note. The song got sadder and the piper began to sniffle. He was a sensitive fellow who in the normal course of life had no great love for dogs, but the dirge brought him down. Overcome with grief and childhood memories, he broke into uncontrollable sobbing and wailing. His sorrow was contagious, and by the third verse Martin Herod was weeping and the country and western band cried shamelessly. Elbib counted sheep to ward off the malady, but even then the little brown collie, wagging tail and licking tongue, leaped around his head. Tom faltered midway through the seventh verse and staggered to the toilet.

When it appeared the dirge had put a cap on the night, the piper suddenly burst into a most melodious song that startled everyone. His voice was gentle and jovial, and so humorous were the verses that he soon had everyone, including Martin Herod, singing in the chorus. And as if she had known the ditty all her life, Mary Ellen harmonized with the piper and Elbib chuckled with delight.

"Well of course," said Pat Patrick, "the piper got great praise and cheers for his song..."

"Ahmm...what was it called...Pat Patrick?" asked Mango Softwood.

"I don't know...but anyway, whatever. Where was I? Yes, anyway the piper made his way over to Elbib to have a few words with him...and to borrow a few pounds from him as well, because the poor divil was broke..."

"A great night sir," lisped the musician, "I hope we are enjoying it."

"Yes indeed. A mighty night...and listen, you are great on these pipes...though I gather little is known about you."

"That is true. I was better known years ago, but that's life. I keep a low profile as they say, from tax men, radio men and the people in Merrion Square."

"Naturally. And of course from *Comhaltas*."

"Now you have it sir."

"You are very wise. But if I may say so, you will not go unnoticed. The spirit you exude is political."

"I don't understand big words, sir."

"Well...what I mean is the special branch will tape your movements. They do that nowadays."

"Very possible...and I hope they enjoy them when they play them back."

"Yes...well anyway, can I treat you to something? Do I remember you drinking cognac?"

"I could be suppin' worse. A drop of brandy will be fine. Thank you very much sir and may the Lord lave you a long time to us."

Elbib called the drink and discreetly slipped a few pound notes into the piper's waiting hand. He lit a cigarette and gave it to the musician.

"But Mister piper, I'd like your opinion on something that's occupying my mind since I came in here tonight."

The piper tilted his head and dragged deeply on the cigarette.

"Shoot," he said.

"Well," continued Elbib, "I was thinking about taking a wife and I was wondering if you have any opinions on the state of marriage, you being a well-travelled person."

"I have no opinions on that matter. But I have, in my time, heard some frightening things about the state, from songs and recitations mainly. I hope it's not an emergency?"

"Lord God no!" chuckled Elbib, patting the piper's shoulder to allay his fears.

"I'm very glad. Very glad indeed. And the best of luck to yourself and the lucky lady. Give her my good wishes when ye meet again. And sir, let me know when the big day is near and I'll drop in for the party. I might even play at the church if the priest agrees, but some of them are wary of me, sir. That's the way with them now."

"You'll be more than welcome."

"And sir, while we're on the subject, a small bit of advice that might make your passage through uncharted waters a small bit easier. Sir, don't spoil the rod and spare the child when the wind is from the south and the moon is on the wane."

"Good advice. Thank you, and speaking of rods and thinking of reels, because that's how the world works, do you by any chance play a jig called 'Out in the Ocean'?"

"Lord Christ, a lovely tune! Molloy makes a great job of it. Would you like to hear it?"

"Yes indeed!" Elbib said, beckoning to Martin to fill a round of drinks for the house.

"You like the old tunes sir," the piper wheezed, "you're like myself. They remind me of long nights in crowded cottages where drink and sweet cake was plenty, long before worry and depression were invented. Back in the times when you could sleep in a damp bed without the fear of catching your death of cold. Ah sir,

'*In Kinvara and Kenmare,*
The West coast of Clare,
From Donegal to Annascaul
And Ballaghadereen
Now seldom seen.'

There's where I soldiered sir."

"Fair play to you," saluted Elbib, "and may blind eyes save you from Charity Meadows."

They clinked glasses in a toast and the piper said, "Thanks sir, and I'll be gone from Miltown Malbay by October First."

"Lovely aul Miltown!" whooped Bachus, topping up the basin with poteen.

"We played with the best of 'em there!" declared Sultan Softwood, rising from his chair.

Elbib nodded and helped the piper steady himself on a high stool. After the ritual checking of the bellows, complaining about the humidity in the bar and the age of the reeds in his pipes, the musician effortlessly tuned the instrument and spat on his hands. Holding the chanter between his long bony fingers, he pumped the wheezing bellows with his elbow, lowered his head and ploughed into the tune.

Martin Herod immediately stopped washing glasses and leaned his head towards the music. It reminded him of something, not the tune itself, but the way it was being played. A vague smile passed his face. He remembered today was the first day of summer and glimpsed into Arcadia. Martin knew this place, hidden birds singing on tree tops, the sleepy river that curled like an eel on the valley floor. The tune brought him back there. Once upon a time, he lingered here on sunny afternoons, leaning against chestnut trees that had sheltered many souls and knew many secrets. He said he could always go back there and find his soul. But he was wrong. When he returned years later the birds did not sing for him, the river ignored him and the big chestnut trees were silent. And when their branches flexed against the cold wind from the water, he sensed anger. Nature has left me, Martin Herod thought in alarm.

"A terrible thought," moaned Pat Patrick, "but you see, he was under a trance with the music and didn't know what was goin' on. Torn between two worlds he was, deserted by both of them. That's the way. Oh my God, the music was great and everyone in the town heard it but couldn't make out where it was coming from or who was playin' it. But they knew they were very good musicianers."

"Fairy music," whispered Ocras Burke.

The piper tripped through the night, accompanied by Elders and Youngers on tambourines and drums, thorn flutes, humming stones, crouds, cruits and mouth pipes. And beneath the path of the music, the world vibrated with the haunting bass notes wrung out by Gleo on an enormous litawn. The temperamental clock which had been mute for hours gently pealed tin ten, tin ten, tin ten, like a lively dancer sporting bells.

"An' then," said Pat Patrick, "what happened, but didn't the rest of the spirits in that very public house appear before Martin Herod and his customers. Right before their very eyes, Elders danced in a ring chantin' and caterwaulin'."

"Holy Mother of all that's good an' holy," whined Martin Herod, blessing himself three times in rapid succession. "Where in the name of Holy Saint Joseph and his blessed mother did these come from? Oh Sacred Heart of Jesus, look down upon us."

He tugged his brother's anchor-like elbow, but Tom growled at him to push off and began clapping to the music.

"Oh Holy Saint Jude, friend of the cornered sinner and unheeded singer...ask Jesus to spare us from this awful cross an' I'll never open this very bar during prayer ever again...please Saint Jude."

Martin fell to his knees behind the counter and crawled to the kitchen for butter, a token he thought might protect him from Them.

"I'll have to call the police," he whimpered. "How did they get in here...Jesus the police...Malone is down. They took him. And they'll take Mary Ellen too...Jesus Christ sure that's why they're here."

In panic he returned to the bar with a pound of salty butter. He watched Mary Ellen dance with Elbib and knew by the sparkle in her eyes that she was taken. They had given her the vision.

The music stopped and Elbib raised his hands.

"Friends and relations and of course our esteemed piper."

"What's he talkin' about?" muttered the musician. "I'm not steamed."

"I'm happy to tell you all that my search for a consort has finally ended."

"Maybe he wants me to play at a concert," mumbled the piper, groping along the countertop for drink, anyone's drink. Bottles and glasses tumbled to the floor and Tom Herod warned him to sit down or be thrown out.

"Martin," called Elbib. "Bring out the bubbly."

Unable to refuse a call for drink, Martin Herod skulked away for the champagne and everyone cheered and clapped. Bottles popped like airguns and ribbons of foam streamed forth. Elders and Youngers toasted Elbib and Mary Ellen while Martin wept in the kitchen, trying to raise the sleeping telephone operator on the black phone.

When he returned to the bar, it was as quiet as a graveyard. Elbib, Mary Ellen, Youngers, Elders and piper were gone. Tom Herod sat at the counter and opened the last button on his shirt.

"Where are they?" stammered Martin.

Tom shook his head and pursed his lips, the sudden silence had stunned him.

"Ask me another, brother," he drawled eventually, "I was looking at the little fellows dance around Dinny MacEarl's daughter and the tall guy and suddenly they vanished with a whoosh." He shrugged his shoulders and said, "It's a new one on me."

"Jesus Christ," moaned Martin, uncorking a whiskey bottle with a squeak. "This is terrible, a right nightmare."

He poured himself a good draught of whiskey and the brothers drank in silence, each thrashing out their own troubles as the early morn crows scavenged the street outside. Tom thought about a young widow in Southie and Martin blamed himself for letting Mary Ellen slip away. In the hope of luring her under his roof, he had served her awkward father countless gallons of free drink and given him numerous never-never loans.

"What's wrong with me?" he asked aloud.

Tom stared at him. The brother's face was creased with worry, ridges gouged his forehead and his eyes were bleary with guilt and shame. Downcast as a pallbearer at the graveside, drowned in the profound thought that he buried part of himself at every funeral. Impatient thumping at the front door brought him to himself.

"Where's my daughter Herod?" roared Dinny MacEarl, striding to the counter.

Martin retreated before him and planted a bottle of rum and a glass between them.

"God...Dinny, I don't know...that time I rang you...she was here... when I got off the phone she was gone."

"Who was she with? Hah?"

Martin and Tom Herod related as much as they could recall of the night's events, neglecting to mention the disappearance of Tanya Lee Low, the gunfire and the mysterious dancers.

"For all I know, she might have got a ride home with the tall fella. Did any car pass you on your way here?" Martin asked timidly.

Dinny grunted.

"Well this is the last time she'll ever come into this joint. Give us the loan of a tenner till I get the creamery check."

Out of habit Martin opened the till, but his fingers felt no money, only leaves, fresh dewy May Bough leaves.

"They often do that," mentioned Ocras Burke, speaking from experience, "leave gold that turns to dust or cow dung in the pocket of the unbeliever."

Martin was still nursing his bewilderment when Seán Lee Low yawned on the floor and raised his head into the grey morning light. Then Malone revived with a puzzled look, quickly settled his policeman's hat on his head, dusted his uniform and struggled to his feet.

"Where's that fellow who was looking for the woman?" asked the sergeant. "I want to question him about a certain incident...and that piper...he's wanted for burning down a house in Galway."

"And my wife?" pleaded Lee Low, "She still gone? Yes?"

Martin remained silent, the questions went over his head and his eyes were on the toilet door, creaking open. He prayed for miracles. He prayed like he had never prayed before...that Mary Ellen would appear and that the night had been a bad dream. But hope and faith fizzled when Tanya Lee Low crawled from the lavatory on her hands and knees, a pool of water trailing behind her. Like a freezing gun dog, she dripped and drooled in the early sunlight that now brightened the bar. Her bellicose bosom bulged with rage and revenge as she approached her distraught husband.

"Well of course," said Pat Patrick, frisking his pockets for cigarettes he did not have. "Seán Lee Low bolted from the pub with his life and hasn't been seen or heard of since."

"That's the truth," confirmed Ocras, giving Pat Patrick a cigarette, "That's the truth, the place is up for sale."

"Of course," continued Pat Patrick, "no wan could make head or tail of the night but they knew it was no good looking for Mary Ellen. No good in this wide earthly world. She was gone with Them and that was the end of the story. But by the same token, and this brings me back to the handkerchief I mentioned early in the night. That handkerchief was dropped by Mary Ellen as she passed over the bridge with Them, for that's the path They take. According to the boy who told me the story, she dropped it to cut her ties with this world."

"Where's the handkerchief now, ahmm Pat Patrick?" asked Sultan Softwood in a meek voice.

"Well, and now this is the best of it. The young man who told me the story asked for it and I hadn't the heart to refuse the cratur. God help us, it seems he was great with her an' they goin' to school. I s'pose he thought it might bring her back to this world again if they ever chanced to meet and he had it in his pocket. Some people say that works, but I don't know...and another thing he told me, wherever he heard this...he said Elbib gave a new name to the girl, *Bláth na Spéire*, Flower of the Sky. There's a new star in the sky since that night. That's a fact, sure I saw it myself."

"I believe it," muttered Bachus.

"There was nothing so strange in that town," yawned Pat Patrick, "since the morning Molly McNamara came downstairs and found two bullocks and a piebald pony in her kitchen. No wan knew who owned them or could say how they got there. All the doors and windows were locked and bolted. Sergeant Malone herded them to the pound and Father Clancy sprinkled holy water on 'em. Some people said they were the souls of Molly's dead relations on their way from Purgatory.

Well, they grazed above in the pound for five days but were always in poor Molly's kitchen in the morn. And on Saint Martin's Day they disappeared and were never seen again. That's true too."

He yawned again, raked the dying fire and coaxed the last drop of poteen from the basin. The cottage kitchen was grey and leaden in the dawn that stalked through the small windows. It was time to be edging away home, or at least to be edging somewhere else. It was time to leave the Sanctuary and face a deflating world. Sleepers and drunkards were revived, bottles were slipped into deep pockets and instruments cased away. With good wishes and blessings, we bade Pat Patrick farewell and promised to call again next month.

It was a chilly morning that had not yet decided whether to rain or shine. We stood for a while in the haggard to find our bearings, have a smoke and a sip to send us on our way.

"Who drank the first bottle of beer in Inagh?" Palem Folan roared at the sky.

His voice bounced from valley to valley, echoed against the Crying Cliffs and brought to the air every bird in the three parishes that had wings to fly. In the east, the sun crawled through the stone grey sky to see who was shouting in her realm and returned to bed again.

"There goes another day," moaned Uaigneas Gallagher.

Revolution

Gerard Downwave wriggled in the armchair and frisked his pockets for cigarettes.

"Everyone is in one kind of jail or the other," he preached. "What Marx had to say is interesting..."

With a sigh, his wife Mabel excused herself from the musty sitting room and left him chattering to Healer Hawkins about revolt and revolution. She politely closed the door and traipsed down the cluttered hallway to the kitchen: eternal darkness and a sink full of dishes.

Mabel sank into an old motor car seat beside the fire with a tumbler of elderberry wine. It eased the pain and mellowed the madness. Revolution, revolution, revolution. Day and night it was nothing but revolution. One time there was no talk about 'the struggle,' no talk about the military. One time there was talk of nothing else but how he would be headmaster when Master Flood retired. Then he would change the world and drift through the town in a glow like Goldsmith.

He was badly shaken when the school board appointed Paddy Lynch to fill the Master's shoes. How could they do this to him? He trained the football team, played the organ in the church and started up the credit union. How could they say, "Sorry Gerard, we feel Lynch is a better man for the job."

For more than a year they lay awake in bed night after night, going over the same old ground. Her head was addled from his stories and theories. He trusted nobody anymore and almost persuaded her there was a conspiracy against him. Mabel saw her husband turn grey in one winter. She saw his eyes change – saw the pupils contract to mere pinpoints and dart with anger. But she really worried when he jolted upright from the pillow one night, babbling feverishly that he was struck by a profound enlightenment. It was then the sirens screamed inside her head.

And that was only the beginning. Not long after Dora was born, the 'visions' began and the house was plunged into hell. Every evening they prayed in the sitting room while he had his visions, and the room was so charged, the children cried. She cried herself and bit her lips, trying to shut out the mad blabber coming from the head of the household. It was around that time she stopped going out.

Father White visited the house when six Sundays in a row Mabel failed to come to the altar rails. She burst into tears and related her months of terror living with the man who played cards with Jesus and John the Baptist every Friday night. The priest sprinkled Holy Water on her and said she needed to pray harder. He was concerned about Gerard and so was the school board – he was relaying his experiences to the pupils.

"Strange spirits dwell when God vacates, Mabel," he said when leaving.

She came to the rails the next Sunday. That was the last time she left the house, the Sunday Gerard interrupted Father White's sermon with a flourish of blue notes on the church organ. He glued everyone to the floor. The priest calmly said, "Gerard, please leave the organ alone."

Gerard continued bleating out sacrilegious scores. Some worshipers twittered, especially those who skulked behind the statues at the back of the church. Most people squirmed and there was a murmur of panic when little Irene Downwave screamed at the organist, "Stop it Daddy!"

The school board dismissed him with a decent pension and the 'visions' stopped. Gerard took to the bed for weeks, weeping in the dark. Later he held public meetings in the Square and canvassed parents to boycott the school. When the dismissed schoolteacher painted slogans on the road, the police arrested him. Gerard spent ten days in the Bridewell and once released, he flew a red flag over the house and immersed himself in revolutionary rhetoric. New words buzzed around the house – fascists, imperialism, colonialism, Trotsky, Lenin, Marx. When people came to visit her in those days they said it would all pass over, like a stubborn cloud. But they would not look her in the eye. Only Biddy Flanagan did that. Biddy would look her in the eye, grip her hands and blurt, "Jesus Mabel, the poor man will never be the same again."

Biddy used to come at all hours of the day and night with a canvas bag of bottles. Elderberry wine. They would sit weeping in the dark kitchen for hours, drinking wine while the house was torn apart by the Downwave children. Mabel knew nothing about Biddy, who just came to the door one day with her bag and said, "Jesus Mabel, I'm sorry for your troubles."

It was time to make another pot of tea for the revolution.

The blinds were drawn and Mabel sat on the broken down sofa. They took no notice of her. Gerard spoke about the printing press he was setting up in the cellar. He would print pamphlets about the way forward, and distribute them outside the church on Sunday mornings. She half listened, half watched the sparks jump from the fire, and knew it would be another winter of making countless pots of tea for the revolution. The comrades would plot and plan. The police would raid the house a couple of times. Mysterious people would come in the night and stay for a while. They might sleep with one of her daughters and vanish into the night at the call of duty. She worried that Irene was pregnant. Another child for the revolution, another grandchild to feed and wash. It seemed to Mabel she was carrying the burden of the revolution on her shoulders. But this was her only part in it – making tea, minding grandchildren and praying it would be all over soon.

"Mabel," Gerard called, "there's a knock on the door."

It was Biddy Flanagan. The women settled in the kitchen and Biddy wept.

"Jesus Mabel," she keened, "I've something terrible to tell you. Gerard slept with Kathleen Mack above in Doyle's the other night. Mary Kate said not to tell you but what could I do?"

She hugged Mabel and prayed for her wayward husband.

"Jesus Mabel, but men can be awful bastards," she said drying tears with her scarf.

"Born bastards."

"Christ Mabel, I've an egg cup of engagement rings in the dresser at home. Give 'em an inch an they'll nail you to the bed."

Mabel said Gerard had not bedded with her for years. She still kept his clothes in the matrimonial bedroom and he changed there in the morning but never at night. He was only a lodger in the house, someone she once had an affair with, he had long ago slipped away as a husband. Gerard was gone, long gone.

"Who's in the parlour with him?" Biddy asked in a whisper.

"Some fellow called Hawkins."

"Oh Sweet Mother of Jesus an' all that's good an' holy...not the Healer Hawkins?"

"Yes."

"Oh Christ! Mabel, that fella's an awful case and he's only startin' out in life. Terrible to the world. They say he has a cure for everythin'...but he's gone from the wire rightly. God help the poor lad, but he'd drink 'til *maidin geal*. He'll make proper shit of the revolution."

"I hope you're right."

"May the Lord Jesus have mercy on Gerard Downwave," Biddy whispered, reaching for her tumbler of elderberry wine. "Like a child Mabel, Christ have mercy on him. The way sure himself and that poor Nixon fella parade around the town at night is only cruel to the world. In an' out of pubs an everythin'...they're just like the gangsters you'd see in the pictures that used come to the town hall long 'go before they burned it down. God help us."

"They search everywhere for the enemy, but the enemy is within themselves, hiding in their souls," Mabel said wearily. It was a line she had read somewhere, and she tried to believe it.

"Tis no life, God help us," Biddy whispered and slipped into tears.

Rain lashed against the kitchen window and Mabel awoke slouched in the old car seat beside the fire. The house coughed and snored. It was well into the night and Biddy was gone. She was angry with herself for getting comatosed again. Elderberry wine. Biddy must have put the rug over her. All these nights ended the same. Oblivion. Life was becoming a crusade of staggers, rise and falls.

Mabel made her way along the hall, stopping by the sitting room to rake the fire. The room smelled of stale cigarettes and musty books and somebody snored on the broken down couch. The Healer Hawkins. Biddy said he had a cure for everything. Mabel looked at him and wondered if he had a cure for loneliness. She was tempted to wake him.

In one sweep Mabel gathered all her husband's clothes from the wardrobe and flung them from her bedroom. From the chest of drawers his mother gave them as a wedding present, she emptied wads of underwear, socks, shirts, vests and woolen cardigans and heaped them on the landing outside the bathroom.

"Revolutions, like charity, begin at home," she muttered.

Mabel opened the window and let night exorcise the room. She undressed and untied her hair, and naked by the window, let the wind whirl around her anxious body. A glint of light on the dressing table caught her eye – the small pewter framed wedding photograph.

Though she could not see his face, she felt Gerard's stare. He was lording over her again, smirking at the naked body he left behind a decade or more ago. A lot of lonely nights had passed through her room since then. Her heart screamed and she thought her body would burst with the rush of blood through her veins. In a wild sweep she hurtled her wedding photograph through the open window. The wind caught it and she heard the glass shatter against the wall.

Mabel Downwave shuttered the window and wondered if the Healer Hawkins was old enough to know that love was a migrant, a good-night kiss at dawn, a sense of wonder in the fray. She dressed her bed with fresh linen and lit a stick of incense she had been saving for years.

The Warrior Carty

The Warrior had enough of the Christmas fair and took cover in Looney's bar. It was empty, dark and cold, still waiting to be strobed by the solstice sun.

"A harmless aul fair," sniffled Bridgey, toting up his bill on a brown paper bag. "Four shillins for the Powers an' three an' sixpence for the bottle a porter...what's that altogether?"

"Seven an' six, Bridgey," said The Warrior, leaving three half-crowns on the red Formica counter. He settled them into a small pile.

"Thanks Bridgey and good luck to you."

"The same to yourself...ahh they have the country ruined...and everythin' is so dear sure..."

"They have this poor country shagged Bridgey. That's about the size of it now."

"'Tis true for you..."

"And what's more, the crowd that's doin' it never fired a shaggin' shot in their life."

"'Tis true for you."

"Anyways," sighed The Warrior, flopping his arms in resignation, "Give us another small whiskey."

"Powers, wasn't it?"

"Powers it is...that's the way now Bridgey. What kind of a Christmas are ye havin' so far?"

"Yarrah...tis quiet. Don't you know yourself now. An' sure today is the big day an' can't you see the way it is. Quiet, sure. You might rise a stir in it yourself above in the Square later on."

"Not today Bridgey."

"No?"

"Not today Bridgey," The Warrior repeated, shaking his head, "but anyways, this is the overcoat I was tellin' you about, the last day I was here."

She admired the dark Crombie coat and listened to how he came upon it. And he was wearing the good blue suit, clean shirt, collar and tie. These he bought from the Pakistani hawker who came to Ennis every Saturday. That was another story, better left for another day, he said.

"Is there anyone dead belongin' to you?" she asked.

"No, not that I know of Bridgey," he answered, "and I didn't hear anything up the town. But there was a funeral this morn beyond in Maheramore, I s'pose you heard that. That poor Mrs. Canney was buried. Her son is married to a daughter of Paraffin Hogan's."

"Is that the boy that drives Blake's lorry?"

"Now you have it."

"That's where Doran's hearse must have been. It passed up the road a while ago."

"I got a lift to town with them. Twas my first time in a hearse and it won't be my last Bridgey."

"Tis true for you."

She smoked one of his cigarettes and put the pieces together. The Warrior was wearing his good clothes because of the funeral. He had a few drinks after filling the grave with Doran. That's why he wasn't going up to the Square, because he had drink taken. He never drinks before going to the Square.

"Are you alright now for a while? I have to put down the dinner."

"Sound as a bell Bridgey – but give us another half wan an' a packet of plain cigarettes so I won't be botherin' you."

Bridgey peeled potatoes into a bowl by the kitchen fire.

"That bar out there is freezin'," she sniffled.

If it got any colder she would have to get an oil heater. She could hear him stamp his feet to keep the blood running to his toes.

"Are you alright, Warrior?" she called, tapping on the bar window.

"Sound as a bell Bridgey. The circulation."

"I hope he don't throw a turn," she mumbled. It would be the talk of the country, The Warrior Carty to die in the only pub he was served in. The six other publicans in the town would not let his toe inside their doors, but Bridgey saw no harm in him. He was persecuted by his own after he fought for them in the War of Independence and the Civil War. Later he went abroad and the misfortunate wretch got shell-shocked in some foreign war. That's where the strange behavior comes from, like the exhibition above in the Square.

"God help us," she sighed and added an extra potato to the pot.

The usual crowd gathered in the Square before midday and waited for The Warrior Carty. This was the highpoint of their fair, to see this robust man lift a cartwheel, which was as big and as heavy as himself, and balance it on the hub of his chin while the Angelus bells rang out. It was an extraordinary feat and they cheered him on. He performed it at every fair, hail, rain or snow, and did it to distract the fair from prayer. He succeeded for the most part, and his act could be the making or the breaking of the day.

When the church bells called for prayer in Looney's bar, The Warrior blew a smoke ring for every peal. It was as defiant as he wanted to be that midwinter's day. He knew the followers in the Square would be disappointed, but that was life: nothing lasts for ever. He had retired. The decision had been made in his sleep and he was obeying. Orders from the Management. Not God, just the Management.

The crowd felt like fools. Cheated of their entertainment and their prayers, they dispersed sullenly and griped about The Warrior. Where was he? Had he not walked the town earlier in the day, showering everyone with Christmas greetings? It was not his form to ignore the call of duty...especially today, the Small Fair of Christmas.

A long lean farmer said he must have lost his nerves. His neighbour disagreed.

"The Warrior was born without nerves," he claimed. "It's his age. He must be sixty-five or seventy years old if he's a day."

They went into Peter Egan's bar and joined a couple of cattle jobbers who were already discussing the Warrior.

"Well sure he started out first in Boland's Mill in 1916...then he led the Faha column of the boys in 1920," declared a barrel-shaped jobber in a once-white coat. "I know it. And he never surrendered after the Civil War. I know that too. Carty never handed over the gun."

"That's right sure. 'Don't give up the fight.' I often heard him say that," drawled his companion. "An' he went off to Spain with the Brigade too. Maybe that was to get another wallop at the Blueshirts."

"Maybe, but I don't think so."

"An' sure if they hadn't locked him up in the Curragh Camp durin' the last war he'd have been soldierin' somewhere."

Bridgey left a plate with a piece of haddock and a potato on the counter.

"Ate this," she said. "It'll do you good."

"The Blessin' of God on you Bridgey," he said and picked at the meal. He felt like confiding in her. He wanted to explain why he didn't go to the Square and what he was doing in Sunday clothes. But it was a delicate matter and she might pick it up wrong.

"Bridgey," he said, motioning for another whiskey and stout, "do we soften with age?"

"Tis hard to say," she said slowly and pondered at her reflection in the mirror behind the whiskey bottles.

"The aul fair'll be over early," she muttered, putting his drinks on the cold red-topped counter. He would be her only customer today.

The money box was getting heavier and he was getting drunker, but in a quiet sort of a way. For a short while, a beam of evening sun warmed the bar and they traced about things of long ago like rekindled lovers. He reminisced about the big fairs, when you could walk on the backs of beasts from one end of the town to the other without stepping on the ground. Bridgey reminded him of the great dances that used to be held before the Christmas, years ago.

"All that's gone now," she sighed.

They recalled the big crowds arriving home from England and wondered where they all were now.

"A sad day for Ireland, Bridgey."

The Warrior sighed and a cloud of silence darkened the bar.

Bridgey fumbled under the counter and a string of Christmas lights blazed a trail around whiskey bottles. Tiny beads of yellow, green, red and blue blinked at The Warrior.

"Jaysus Bridgey," he said slowly, "but I love Christmas, even though Christmas is not the same as it used to be."

"Nothing stays the same sure," she said, almost in a whisper.

Sipping a cup of tea, she peered at him from the dark kitchen. He was talking to himself and counting his money, cursing her blinking Christmas lights. The Warrior had enough drank for one day but she hated to ask him to leave. He tapped the counter with the heel of his glass and called her.

"The same again Bridgey...is that clock right?"

"No...tis slow...hurry up an' finish this like a good boy. Tonight's the night of the carol singin' above at the church an' I must get ready."

"Sound Bridgey. An' Bridgey, before I forget it...give us a naggon of whiskey and a packet of Players for the morn."

"Here," she said, wrapping the small bottle and cigarettes in a brown paper bag, "this is from me for Christmas."

He pressed his chest against the counter and lowered his head as if to kiss her. But he clasped her cold hands instead and whispered, "You never forget the Warrior. The blessin' of God on you. Bridgey, you're the only wan in this town who has any breedin'."

"You can't bate breedin', Warrior," she said. "How're you goin' home?"

"The bicycle."

She came outside the counter with a broom and peered out the front door.

"There's no wind out. Take it aisey an' you'll be sound."

"I'll be sound anyway...But Bridgey as the song goes, 'Oh what matters when for Erin dear we fall.' I don't mind in the least fallin' for Erin...many's the good man an' woman have done so in the past. But

Bridgey, what I do mind, is fallin' for some of the shaggers that live here."

"Our Lord fell three times," she said quietly, sweeping his crushed cigarette butts into a heap.

"And he rose again Bridgey. We're martyrs for punishment."

The Warrior drained his glass slowly and put Bridgey's Christmas present into his overcoat pocket. He wondered if he should try for another half one, but decided not to, it would be bad form.

"Bridgey...I'll hit away," he said. "Happy Christmas and a prosperous New Year to you *astore*."

"The same to yourself and be as good as you can Warrior. Happy Christmas to you now. Mind the step as you g' out."

She bolted the door behind him and unplugged the Christmas lights.

Main Street smelled like a farmyard in the wake of the fair. It was quiet, apart from a few children who played in the light streaming from Callaghan's sweet shop. The town was winding down for the carol service and The Warrior growled when he discovered the pubs were blacked out. He tried them all: Tracy's, Egan's, Hogan's, Vaughan's, The Widow's and Dinn Joe's.

"Shag 'em," he swore, "an' shag 'em again."

He had hoped to breeze into the enemy camp in the quiet of the evening, just when the day's takings were counted and the publicans were happy. He would extend the olive branch and ask to be served again. He would keep the peace. There would be no more trouble, no more defiance. No more would he lure the Christians away from the Angelus prayer by balancing the cartwheel. He was retiring from all that.

But his plan was foiled; he had tarried too long with Bridgey. And the church didn't help. The pubs would be closed until after the carol singing. Muttering about goodwill and room at the inn he plodded back down the street to wait in the shadows until God relented.

Passing Peter Egan's he had a sudden urge to lash his boot through the glass paneled door but was distracted when the new curate, Father Hannon, suddenly appeared like a host.

"Hardy weather," the pale priest hailed, side-stepping him.

"Say wan for me Fader," grunted The Warrior and wandered in the opposite direction.

He slipped into Hogan's Alley to relieve himself in the darkness, but Gretta Greene saw him. The mad woman from Frohaul who had once done him a turn behind the town hall peered into the laneway and jeered, "The frost 'll kill et. The frost'll kill et an' make a small boy of you Warrior Carty, you dirty scut you. I'll say a prayer that you'll go ta hell."

With his back to the church he plodded on. Two women, pious as nuns, scurried past, arm in arm.

"Peggy, is that the Warrior Carty?"

"'Tis. He's an awful nuisance."

"He's in town since early today. I saw him when I was gettin' the paper. Was there a girl in that family?"

"No. An only child that fella, an' spoiled an' he young. He lives on his own. The mother died in the workhouse. Sure that fella couldn't take care of himself."

"Never married?"

"No, and he let a great farm of land go to wrack 'n ruin. Drank it."

The Warrior felt the cold in his bones. Frost glistened the black tar road that separated the lines of shops. Stars above and stars below. He stood at the Square and gazed at the sky. A great black dome dotted with peep holes to heaven. Shocked by the thought, his head reeled.

"Jaysus...I'm half drunk," he mumbled to the night. "I'd better sit down before I keel over."

Outside Hogan's pub he flopped on an empty porter barrel. Hogan would be his first port of call with the olive branch, the whiskey would keep him warm till then. He uncorked the naggon and listened to the Christmas carols escaping from the church. Some he knew from long ago and crooned along between sips of whiskey. Memories paraded before him and he felt the town growing strange. It reminded him of a desolate railway station he saw from a train, one winter evening in war-torn Spain.

"I'm only just passing through," he muttered.

After the carol singing, the faithful passed The Warrior slouched over the empty barrels outside Hogan's.

"He's in town all day," a man from the Vincent de Paul whispered to his wife.

"Thank God you don't drink," she whispered back. "It's a terrible curse."

Father Hannon shook his head and crossed to the other side of the street.

"An awful disgrace," he muttered to Coyne the butcher.

Nobody bothered The Warrior and hard frost crept over his Crombie coat in a white fur. At closing time Frank Hogan tried to move him on, not out of sympathy or concern, but out of fear that the old soldier might erupt during the night and cry him out. But the old soldier was dead. Twisted like a vine, white with ice, The Warrior was gone and only his burly body remained.

His remains were brought to the church in a plain coffin paid for by Bridgey Looney and Ned Duffy. Laid out in his good blue suit he looked like a saint in death. After Mass on Christmas morning only a few mourners followed the tricolor-draped coffin through the streets. The Christmas morning cap guns were silent, the children called a truce for the funeral.

It was bitter cold in the graveyard above the town and Father Hannon rushed through the prayers. Ned Duffy fired four shots from an old revolver and children in the town below replied with a thousand rounds or more.

"Home is the hero," Bridgey whispered. "May God be good to you, Warrior Carty."

Derramore

Turbo Tracy was as welcome as the cuckoo in the West, his arrival was a sign of heady times down the road. In the pubs and shops you would overhear people say, "Somewan was tellin' me Turbo Tracy is around. He was beyond in Trá Rue sellin' greyhound pups last week."

"Well if he is, they could be lucky pups. Steam will be let off somewhere."

Like when all the casks of brandy were washed ashore in Barr Trá. Turbo had arrived a week before, flogging glass tumblers. Another time he was around selling 'magic numbers' that you sent to Dublin and money came back in the post. The summer he had the job playing the piano in Gordon's Hotel, he ended up riding Mamie's horse past the winning post for eight races on the trot and everyone made a small fortune.

But Turbo's presence did not bring a smile to everyone's face. Authorities viewed him as the advance party for chaos and he made clergymen fidgety and officials alert. Anarchy in the wind.

A lone operator, like the cuckoo, Turbo kept his distance from the authorities, but when his back was turned, they were sniffing at his heels. He would protest and say that whatever turmoil there was on heaven or earth, he was not the cause of it, just a symptom. They had an ingrained fear that somewhere, some time, Turbo Tracy would arrive hawking fireworks the day after the safety match caught on. As it turned out, it was the matches he brought.

One Garland Saturday, the last Saturday in July, he came to St. MacDara's Well with the intention of peddling religious emblems and relics to the people there on pilgrimage. He set up a green canvas-covered stall a short distance from the holy well and cranked up an old gramophone. To attract attention, he played vaudeville songs from New York.

"Photographs of St. Patrick at great expense from the New World!" he hailed. "Medals of the Pope, Matt Talbot and Canon Matthews. Relics from Rome guaranteed for life..."

People crowded to the stall but dismissed his offerings.

"No, no," they said, "we have them things at home."

They listened and ogled at the singing box. Then he abruptly stopped the music and raised his hands.

"Alright my friends!" he called, "Happy Garland to ye all."

"Happy Garland Turbo!" and a chorus of cheers.

"There's no demand for medals. Ye want music! Times are changing! How nice! But I can't play it for naught. Never did. Never will. This machine costs much money and it eats a lot..."

More cheers.

"It's true...but as ye know, Turbo Tracy was always a generous man..."

"With his flute!" piped someone.

Raucous laughter and cat calls.

"Now, now, not nice talk near holy water!" snapped Turbo, "So people, if ye want music ye'll have to pay for it."

He took off his black beaver hat and placed it open mouth on the counter.

"Come by the hat, drop in your change and I'll oblige."

In the background, the murmur of prayer rose from the well. Nobody ventured to the hat and there was a certain uneasiness, with begrudgers casting crude remarks at the dapper little peddler. But when he raised a few medals and hailed, "Medals of the Pope, Matt Talbot and Canon Matthews," a couple of people rushed from the shadows and money jingled into the hat. More followed and he gave them music.

That calm summer's night, Tracy's gramophone music was heard in three parishes, and country people who had no intention to trek to the well for prayer were hoodwinked there by the curious noise. By the time Father White arrived, St. MacDara's Well was a swarm with boisterous men, women and young adults shuffling under a full moon to the saucy crooning of Al Jolson. The priest ripped the disc from its spin and silenced the night.

"Oh shyte," moaned some drunk, "it's Fadar White."

"Sinners!" cried the clergyman, "Sinners! At a place of prayer, you have sinned!"

"Now now holy man," darted Turbo, "music is a gift of the Gods."

"How dare you interrupt me!" he snapped. "And this is more sin!"

He held up a handful of Tracy's medals and relics.

"Simony! Have ye forgotten the words of the Lord Jesus? Have ye? Do ye hear me? I hope he forgives ye."

In one sacrificial move, he lifted the gramophone over his head, crashed it on the ground and slouched away muttering in Latin.

"You'll pay for that, you spoil sport!" roared Turbo.

Smarting from the priest's ire, the crowd melted away into the darkness. Cowering like small animals in the shelter of walls and bushes, they watched Turbo abandon his stall and head for Barnagweeha.

A few days later, when Father White called on Mrs. Penny Wyse of the Elms, he was startled to see Turbo stretched on a deck chair on the front lawn. He scurried around the back of the house, a thousand thoughts colliding in his head. Penny was picking strawberries and waved when he appeared.

"Father Tom! How lovely to see you! Just in time for some strawberries and cream."

"Penny," he said urgently, "what is Turbo Tracy doing here?"

"Who?"

"Turbo Tracy. The man lounging on the deck chair outside."

"Oh! Boney you mean! Isn't he a dear!"

Father Tom shook his head vigorously,

"Penny," he said, "that's Turbo Tracy...he's no addition to anyplace."

"What's the matter Father Tom? Is there something I should know?"

They adjourned to the conservatory and the priest told her all he knew about Turbo over a glass of gin. It was an unhealthy sign to see his likes in the district. He cropped up every few years like a bad penny, always hawking something. The last time Turbo was around he was selling women's underclothes. Another time he passed through with a bale of green tobacco that turned half the province into dreamers.

Penny sighed and explained that he was lodging with her. He was so cheeky, a proper little wagtail. And at this hour of his life, at least sixty five years old and yet no fear in him of God nor man. She thought he was a writer, a collector of folktales and folklore.

"He told me his name was Turlough Bonaparte Tracy...if I had any idea he was called Turbo I would not have let him under my roof. What a ghastly name – Turbo! But he seemed such a nice man."

"How long is he staying?"

"Three weeks. He paid in advance. He wanted the annex because it has a study off the bedroom and overlooks the garden. He's working on something, he said. Well I never."

"I wonder what. Watch him Penny...you never know with his type. Anyway, I was calling to discuss the gymkhana."

They talked about the gymkhana, but Turbo had cast a shadow on the day. His name cropped up in the midst of horses-talk and he became the focus of conversation again. Penny knew the priest did not approve of her lodger, but money was scarce at the Elms ever since Elliott Wyse left without saying good-bye.

"What can I do?" she asked. "It's not been a great year for visitors, you know."

Father White understood. He took her hand and said, "Just be careful Penny. A man like Tracy can cause havoc. Anyway I have a few more calls to make."

On his way back to the parochial house that evening, he called at the police barracks and reported Tracy's whereabouts to Sergeant Turner.

Over the next couple of weeks, Turbo only left the Elms to go to the post office or slip down to Egan's for a few whiskeys. He always locked his quarters going out. Penny watched him, but kept out of his way. When he told her he wanted to stay another month at the Elms, she said cooly, "Mr. Tracy, I want to have a word with you. Sit down please."

"Smoke?" asked Turbo, offering her a slim cheroot.

Penny Wyse shook her head and said, "I've been hearing upsetting things about you."

Turbo raised his grey eyebrows and listened to his landlady beat around the bush. His face twitched. When she finished he said, "There's two sides to every story and a thousand versions of every song. Anyway, Mrs. Wyse I would not dream to pass another night where I am not welcome. That would interfere with my work."

"For heaven's sake! What work?"

Turbo shook his head and rose from the chair.

"You wouldn't understand," he said distantly. "You wouldn't understand. I'll pack my things and look for a room down the town."

She watched him briskly climb the stairs and thought he was an agile man for his age. His brain was always working, she could see it in his eyes and it struck her that he might have been in a seminary, possibly the Jesuits. A spoiled priest, that might be why Father Tom was wary of him. He was a mystery with a history, of that she was sure.

He was packing when she knocked on the annex door.

"May I come in?" Penny asked sheepishly.

"It's your house," he muttered.

"You don't have to leave right away, you know. Your rent is paid until Sunday."

He ignored her and continued packing. Rain spattered on the window and the grey house turned cold.

"Look," she said, sitting on the bed, "I may have overreacted. It's not been easy for me since Elliott walked out of here. Sometimes I get carried away..."

Turbo shook his head and sighed. He had met countless Pennys in his travels, down-at-heel West Britons who lived in big empty houses, full of memories and gloomy portraits. Aspirations of grandeur, a haughty accent and a leather saddle. Blow-ins who changed with the wind.

"Look, Mr. Tracy, I'm sorry if I upset you. Please stop packing. You can stay for as long as you like."

"Time to go."

"I'd like it if you stayed. I like to have a man around the house. Please reconsider Mr. Tracy. Please."

She left the room and Turbo yawned. That woman is bats, he thought. Rashers sizzled in the kitchen below and the warm smell of bacon sought him out. He stopped packing and lay on the bed, listening to the rain. It was no evening to be looking for lodgings.

When Father White called the following week, he heard that Turbo had extended his tenancy. The priest pursed his thin lips and shook his ears.

"He's well off from what I can see," Penny ventured.

"Well off! Penny! What's he doing?"

"He's writing a book," she bluffed. She liked to fantasize about her house guests.

"I know he writes a lot of letters Penny, I often see him go to the post office."

"A horrendous amount of letters. But nobody writes back to the poor soul. Writing is such a lonely business."

She said he was very scholarly and thought he might have considered law or the church as a career in his youth. He had that look in his eye. Father Tom frowned. Had she forgotten all he told her about this vagabond? He sensed she might be getting soft on Tracy and spoke cryptically about temptations of the flesh. He was a charmer he said, and Penny smiled. She liked to see the priest worked up.

"What about a nice glass of gin?" she said seductively.

All Turbo's letters were answered at once and in the same week, eight small twine-tied parcels arrived at the Elms for him. Squirrel-like he scampered to his room with them and when Penny politely asked what was coming into her house he said, "Money from heaven."

She smiled, it was nice to see him happy. Nice to have a happy man about the house. Not that he was very good company. He never spoke except when asked something, and he spent most of the time in his room. But she was getting used to him and wondered if they might get closer sometime. He might even winter at the Elms. Even stay for Christmas. Her mind raced and she wondered if he preferred turkey or goose. She began addressing him as Turlough instead of Mr. Tracy.

Penny was unaware her lodger had begun printing money on a small hand press in the annex. When she heard him rummaging upstairs, her husband came to mind and she would sit in the library and read over newspaper clippings about his disappearance. For weeks before Elliott fled from the house, he rummaged in the attic, keeping her awake most of the night. Then one morning early, the front door banged shut and when she came down stairs, she sensed he had left forever.

"The rotten bastard," she spat, "the cheek of him."

That was years and years ago and her anger was long since burned out. She was only sorry for the years wasted thinking he would come back.

By October, Turbo was working day and night and only left his room to trot downstairs for meals and trot back up again. Mrs. Wyse worried about him and mentioned to Father Tom, "He's gone as white as a sheet and he's up most of the night."

"What's he doing Penny?"

"Writing all the time, it seems to me. His fingers are always covered in ink."

"How can he afford to stay this long?"

"A son in Limerick sent him money a while back. It appears the son is in the shipping business. Very well off from what I can gather."

"Money for old rope," Father Tom said cynically. "Baffling. Anyway, what I came to see you about was..."

"The Hunt!"

"You took the words out of my mouth."

"Oh dear! I was only looking at my calendar this morning and thought – imagine it's that time of year already!"

They both laughed and Penny poured two stiff gins.

Usually she did not dine with her lodgers (or guests as she called them), but one morning before Halloween, Penny joined Turbo for breakfast. She chatted about the weather and hoped it would be fine for the next while. Turbo nodded.

"The Hunt meets here on Tuesday next and I can't believe it's that time of the year already. The years just fly as you get older. Do you find that?"

Turbo nodded. They ate in silence for a while and then Penny said in a quiet voice, "You don't look well Turlough. You're working way too hard."

He poured another cup of tea and sighed.

"You should take it easier," she said softly, "a day with the Hunt would do you all the good in the world. I could get you a mount if you wanted to ride with us on Tuesday. You would enjoy the company and a day in the fresh air."

A lot of very interesting people would be riding with them. The Hamiltons and Lord Greenford, Captain Nightwood and Major Wilson. Lady Anne Mountgomery, Fanny Power, Alice Cunningham-White. He would love Alice. She rambled on and told a couple of tally-ho stories. Turbo shook his head and looked agitated.

"Well at least you'll join us for the party afterwards," she insisted. "We have a fancy dress at the Elms every Halloween after the Hunt."

Turbo had visions of the house being invaded by freaks in disguise. He shook his head quickly and said, "Actually I'm hoping to spend Halloween with my son in Limerick. It's his birthday."

"Oh. A Scorpio."

"Indeed."

"What age is he?"

"Thirty-five."

"Well that's nice."

He nodded, dabbed his mouth with his napkin and excused himself from the table.

Turbo lost track of the days and on Tuesday morning, the hunting horns blew him from the bed.

"Damn it!" he cried, "I should be in Limerick since yesterday!"

Crusty accents filled the house. He heard Penny shouting orders and lovely-to-see-yous. Someone said she looked as fresh as a daisy, Penny replied it was all the saddle. The Elms bayed. Outside, hounds barked and yelped. Gravel crunched beneath boots and hooves. Hunters swarmed on the grounds and the chilly morning smelled of leather and horse manure. Turbo pulled the blankets over his head and wished the foxes luck. He rocked in the bed until the noise disappeared over the hills.

Later that day he went to book a seat to Limerick on the mail car. No car until Friday, he was told, two-day service at this time of the year. Friday was fine, it would give him time to get his business in order. He would spend the weekend in the city and return on Monday. On his way back to the Elms he shivered at the thought of horsey people galloping around the house and nipped into Egan's for a whiskey.

Turbo stepped into a nightmare when he returned half-loaded to the Elms that night. The house walked with people in all sorts of costumes, everyone barking like beagles. Keeping close to the wall, he slid through the hall and was about to climb the stairs when he heard Penny cry, "Turlough! I thought you were gone to Limerick! How good to see you! Come and join us!"

He turned around. She was dressed as a clown, white powdered face, red tomato nose and red horse lips.

"Bed time. Well past bed time," he slurred from the second step of the stairs.

"Turlough, don't be a spoil sport! Come and meet the people."

The party goers stared at him. It was Turbo Tracy himself.

"Tally ho!" Father White shouted and they bellowed with laughter as the little man stumbled to the annex.

Turbo was too drunk to undress and fell asleep in his clothes. The mayhem and music below could not bust his nightmare about emptying ditches with a thimble. He snored on even when Florence St. Claire screamed that he had been robbed. That silenced the party. Penny stood up on a chair and pleaded, "Everyone! Let there be no panic! Take a good look around you. It's a beige pigskin wallet. It's here somewhere."

Florence swore it was lifted from the fishing bag he had around his shoulder while dancing. How much had he in it? Enough, he said, but that was not the point, it was of sentimental value. The house was scoured, but no wallet was found. The Halloween party trembled to a murmur. Penny was very upset and wept in the conservatory with Father Tom.

Turbo passed several forged ten pound notes in Limerick and spent extravagantly. Using the name Dr. Wyse, he booked into the Irish Arms, cutting a fine dash in his new cape, soft hat, dark suit, gold pocket watch and matching cuff links. He traveled by hackney around the city, tipping heavily. In the evenings he mingled with dockers and sailors in the Albatross, sniffing for contraband and banned books. At night he drank brandy and played poker with local sharks who called him Doctor. He made it clear he was not a medical doctor, but a doctor of literature. They were more impressed when he showed them a heavy book called *Ulysses*.

He was glad to be leaving Limerick on Monday morning, before he made a dent in the economy. Sharing the seat in the mail car with him back to Barnagweeha was a man who introduced himself, "You must be Turbo Tracy, I'm Gerard Downwave."

"Huh? I am Turlough Bonaparte Tracy, or Mr. Tracy. Not Turbo, Tarbert or Turbot."

"Sorry about that. You're stayin' up at the Elms. How's Penny?"

"As good as a landlady can be."

"Christ but she's very affected. D'you know, the haughty-taw accent and all that aul shit."

Turbo waved his hand for an end to conversation, but Downwave continued, "Father White spends a lot of time up there with ye. That fella'd get up on a cat. But what does he be doin' up there with Penny? Hah? She's no angel herself either. I suppose you know that she was mixed up in that scandal with Howard MacDonald and the wife."

"Naw, naw, naw," moaned Turbo, waving his hand.

"White got all that hushed up. He was caught with Howard's wife too. Hah? Sure that's why they call him the White Lie. Christ, that was a lousy thing he did to your gramophone back at the well last Garland."

"Ah shag him!" exploded Turbo.

He reached for a flask of whiskey he had for the journey and drank away without offering it to his traveling companion. Downwave didn't notice and veered into a monologue about revolution and undermining church and state.

"Jesus Christ!" spat Turbo, squinting at his pocket watch, "Since I got on this carriage two hours ago, I've heard more talk about revolution than I heard all the rest of my life. And I'm not a young man. Shut up for the love of your country."

There was nothing else said. For the remainder of the journey, Turbo drank and Downwave slept. When the mail car halted outside the post office, Tracy was so drunk he refused to believe they had reached Barnagweeha. Downwave convinced him they were home after ten minutes or so and helped him to the Elms with his parcels and boxes. Penny was startled to see her boarder return drunk.

"Bring him into the drawing room, there's a fire on," she said to Downwave without looking at him, "I'll make some soup."

"Thank you, thank you. Christ I'm loaded."

"You're grand," consoled Downwave.

Mrs. Wyse nursed Turbo with hare soup. She asked about his son and he said that he would be moving nearer to him in the New Year.

"I'll miss you, Turlough," said Mrs. Wyse, and Downwave nodded in agreement.

"Sorry to hear that," mumbled Turbo rising from the chair.

He staggered against the table and Downwave rushed to support him.

"Jesus. Give me a hand up the stairs, will you?" he mumbled to Downwave.

It was a slow climb, Penny watching from below. Turbo was footless, she had never seen anyone dressed so well being so drunk, apart from that wealthy doctor who used to visit the Hamiltons in Glenbay House. And she did see Mitchland the Chemist fairly sodden one Christmas... Mitch was a natty dresser. She heard Turbo jingle his bedroom door key. The bed creaked and boots hit the floor. Downwave asked if he was alright. A couple of minutes later the aide came down stairs smiling.

"He's some character Mrs. Wyse."

"A lovely man."

"He's here with you since Garland, hah. What does he do all the day?"

"He's writing a book about his life," she said.

"Bullshit Penny. That man is a gangster, a right bloomin' trimmer."

"I beg your pardon Mr. Downwave. No crooks sleep under my roof."

And then she thought about St. Claire's wallet and wondered if he knew .

"Ahh Christ Penny...I didn't mean it like that...no, no, what I meant was that he's a bit of a rogue."

"He's in a good town."

"But Christ Penny, he's well off."

"Very," she said sharply. "And now Mr. Downwave, I will see you to the door. Thank you for helping Mr. Tracy home."

Turbo rose two days later, sporting a new tweed jacket and dove grey hat. Penny smelled money and danced around him. He grunted and asked if there was mail for him.

"No, but Gerard Downwave called here and asked that you go up to his house as soon as you can."

"Who?"

"Downwave. The man who was here with you the other night. You came home together in the mail car."

"Oh that anti-Christ. I've no business with him. No business with him."

Penny shook her head and laughed,

"Oh Turlough, you're such a darling."

Downwave was annoyed when Turbo failed to call after a week, so he marched up to the Elms and asked to see him. Penny said her lodger was still sick from his trip to Limerick and could not be disturbed. Downwave whipped an envelope from nowhere and said, "Give him that and tell him I'll be back in half an hour."

When he returned she ushered him into the drawing room.

"You should be ashamed of yourself for upsetting an old man like that," she said. "Mr. Tracy will see you in a while."

Turbo was pale, he smoked a thin cigar and looked around the parlor anxiously. Downwave stretched in an armchair, shoes off, toes to the fire.

"Turlough. You're off color"

"Alright!" Turbo barked. "What do you want?"

"You saw the piece of the ten pound note in the envelope. I know you're forging them upstairs."

Downwave took a handful of ten pound notes from his pocket.

"They're good, I picked them up the night I helped you to bed. Here. You can have them back."

"Keep 'em, Frisky Fingers. Shove 'em. Just don't pass them 'til I've left town."

"How are you goin' to get rid of them Turlough?" asked Gerard in a friendly voice. "You have a couple of boxes of them upstairs. You must have a hundred thousand pounds or two up there."

"None of your business."

"So you passed them in Limerick, hah? You could get a long stretch in the cage for a racket like this. Especially and the country broke."

"Come on, come on. What's on your mind man?" snapped Turbo.

Gerard trotted off into revolution and the old man tired, shielding his eyes and ears from explosions.

"Alright," he sighed, "so you want me to pay you for your silence and this money will go towards your revolution. Is that right?"

"Correct."

"Well bollix to you. I'd prefer to wipe my arse with the money than give it to a misguided politico. Now get to blazes out of my sight and watch for smoke from the chimney. Come on, shag off out of here."

"Hold it Turlough," cried Downwave. "You're takin' me up wrong... I'm only here to give you a hand."

Downwave explained to him a plan he had conceived. There was no bank in the town and though it took a while, all the money in circulation ended up in the hands of a few people, Mr. Hamilton the landlord, Mr.

Morrison the merchant, and Father White. Nobody liked giving them money and Downwave said Turbo's money could be unloaded on them in one huge sweep.

"It'd wipe them out," he chuckled. "Get all of the bastards at once."

"And what will I get? The firing squad?"

"You'll get three pounds for every tenner and the movement will trade the notes at a fiver. That way we all gain – you, the masses and the movement. Naturally you'll be offered a seat on the revolutionary council."

"Shag your revolutionary council, Robin Hood. Get out and watch for white smoke going up the chimney."

"Well you might as well burn them and run for cover. But don't go to Limerick because the game is up there. If the law don't get you the Confraternity will."

Downwave held up one of the notes and said with a grin, "Mr. Tracy, do you see this...the wrong date is on it, your money is a year too soon."

"Whatzat?" He plucked the note from him and held it to the daylight. "Shite!" he shrieked and rushed to his room.

Downwave tossed the notes in the fire and laughed until Penny stormed into the room and asked him to leave.

Turbo cursed and swore for hours in the annex. When Penny knocked on his door he cursed her too, and she was startled but moved by his anger. She knew it had to do with Downwave and it was a crisis. Downwave was a troublemaker. He tried to organize the farmers to block the Hunt only two weeks before and now had the cheek to walk into her house like a friend. Everything Downwave did was sudden and uncomfortable. He wanted revolution, like the one in Russia or better still the one in France. He wanted public blood, oceans of it, he said one time at a meeting in the Square. The police arrested him afterwards. She felt chilly.

Turbo wept in bed.

"After all my work," he keened. "Jesus, after all my work. After a lifetime of planning and ground work, that shagger Kennedy. The clot put the wrong date on the plate. The shagging clot! And I the bigger ass not to cop it. Jesus Christ, what a terrible cock up."

But worse than that, he moaned, he had passed notes in Limerick.

"Oh what a fool, what a fool," he chattered.

The word would certainly be out about him now. They might trace him to Barnagweeha, the name Wyse, he used it at the hotel where he sported and stayed. And now Downwave was into his life...try not to panic, not to panic. We got out of squeezes before, he said to his guardian angel.

"Where there's a will there's a way," his angel whispered. "Let it settle for a while. Relax."

Turbo took up *Ulysses* and went along with it for two days.

"Christ," he said, "this book will distract millions."

He left the tome behind him in the lavatory and decided to cut a deal with Downwave.

After dark, he slipped down to Peter Egan's and discovered in a roundabout way where the anarchist lived. The house stank of nappies and ox head soup. Turbo declined to have a seat in the tar black sitting room. Downwave sprawled on the broken-down sofa and slurped baked beans with a spoon.

"When can you launder this money for me," the forger asked.

"That depends on how much there is. It'll have to be counted, checked out and passed by the council."

"How long."

Two weeks, maybe three Downwave said. Their own funds would have to be assessed, the off load had to be planned. There were lots of details to be attended to. He would call to the Elms in a day or two with word.

Turbo did not sleep that night but neither did Penny. She had found *Ulysses* in the lavatory and was romping through it. When Turbo moped down to breakfast the next morning she was ecstatic.

"Turlough!" she cried. "Where in heaven's name did you pick up this book!"

"The Albatross. Limerick," he muttered.

"Did you read it?"

"Just a little bit."

"Its absolutely shattering!"

He had Joyce for breakfast. Penny was sure she was Molly Bloom she said excitedly. He nodded and felt like talking to her, misfortune had made him lonely for company. Resistance was low at times like this. Temptation and distraction were not fought, but indulged. A watery smile crossed his face.

"Turlough! I have never seen you smile before. But what a sad smile you have."

"I have a blue smile, Mrs. Wyse," he said.

"Turlough, what has Downwave done to you," she asked suddenly.

"Nothing! Nothing at all. We disagree on a philosophical point. That's all."

"I don't like to see him calling to my house, do you know what I mean? He makes my skin crawl. He's a madman."

Turbo nodded and Penny told him about the rise and fall from grace of Gerard Downwave. The story took a few hours to tell and she finished it in the drawing room over a bottle of gin. By evening they were the best of friends, swapping stories before a log fire. Mrs. Wyse yawned and talked about having a nap. Turbo yawned and said he was tired himself.

"Would you like a hot water bottle in your bed," she asked, "to take the chill from the sheets."

"Good idea. Great idea."

Suddenly his knees began to knock franticly.

Early next morning, Gerard Downwave hammered on the door. Penny came down in her dressing gown.

"Is Tracy up yet? Tell him I'm here. It's urgent."

He marched past her and into the drawing room.

"Aristos!" he snarled.

She heard him rake the fire and throw a log or two on the embers. Alarmed, she rushed to the annex.

"Turlough," she whispered, shaking him gently, "Downwave wants to see you."

"Huh?"

"Downwave, darling."

"Downwave! Oh that bastard. Right, right."

Gerard had not shaved for a few days and his eyes were sunken. Turbo thought he was looking more sinister.

"I came to count the loot," he said hoarsely.

The count took Downwave several hours and Turbo paced around the annex chewing cigars.

"Seventeen thousand, six hundred and eighty four notes...all tenners."

Turbo nodded. About a thousand notes were badly forged, Downwave said, he would not be caught dead with them. Turbo flushed.

"Bollix to you!" he sniffled. "The fire, into the fire they're all going and shag you and your revolution."

"This money will burn by itself, it's so hot."

Turbo was flustered. Wads of notes bursting into flames jumped into his mind.

"Alright. The lot for twenty grand," he sighed.

"Fifteen. Remember the cause."

Turbo rolled his eyes,

"When man? When? I have to leave this week."

"Take it handy Turbo, sorry...I meant Turlough. We'll take it in five batches. First one tomorrow morn. I'll have three grand for you. Alright?"

Turbo nodded,

"Now get out of here. Out! Out!"

It was dusk the following evening when Downwave came to the Elms. Turbo was dozing in the drawing room, tired from waiting. Gerard shook his head, bad news, he said, he could only come up with five hundred pounds. Turbo's jaw fell. What kind of messing was this? The ass was more trouble than he was worth. He was setting him up.

"Out! Out! Out!" he barked.

"Take it handy!" snapped Downwave, tossing a plump wallet at him. "This is only the start, you'll have the rest tomorrow."

Turbo dabbed his forehead and temples. Five ton. Half a loaf is better than no bread, he thought, and retrieved from the annex five hundred forged tenners for the revolution.

Dressed in his finest, Turbo drank too much brandy in Egan's that night and staggered home singing. At Honan's Mill he was accosted by Sergeant Turner but ignored the lawman until the song was aired.

"And that's the very reason why I left ol' Skibereen," he warbled in a gravel voice that brought heads to every window in the street.

Turner grabbed his elbow and escorted him to the police barracks in Clare Street.

The sergeant was delighted with his prize. Turbo Tracy had stepped through loopholes from him for years. But red-handed he caught him! Drunk and disorderly, breaking the peace, refusing to cooperate with an officer of the law – all the trappings of a public nuisance. He ordered Turbo to turn out his pockets and when the plump pigskin wallet tumbled on the table his eyes widened.

"'Hello, hello, what have we 'ere?"

"We have a sow's ear," replied Turbo.

Tracy said he bought the wallet from an Asian trader in Mayo and Turner nodded, writing it all down.

"And you'd swear to this?"

"Naturally."

"I'm locking you up for the night," Turner said, "to get you used to a hard bed."

Penny waited up most of the night for the lodger and next morning she knew a crisis had occurred when she heard the rapping on the door. Father White was ashen faced, his eyes were surly and he swallowed hard.

"Penny," he said, wiping his feet on the doormat, "I bring bad news. Your lodger was arrested last night and in his possession was Florence St. Claire's wallet."

"I don't believe it! Oh my dear God!"

She recoiled and threw her hands over her heart.

Father Tom sighed. Turner had called on him earlier and asked to break the news to her. The police would be arriving to search Tracy's quarters later, with her permission.

"God only knows what he got up to while he was here," he said, avoiding her eyes.

"Well of all things. St. Claire's wallet."

"It adds up, Penny. Remember he went away a few days after the incident and came back like Lord Muck. I told you to watch him. Months ago I said that."

"Yes, yes," she said heavily, "You're always right Tom. You never make mistakes like the rest of us."

She wept with her back to him and after a few minutes he sighed and left the Elms.

Penny entered the annex with a master key. Nothing in the bedroom but a battered trunk full of shoddy clothes. She peeked into the study and banged the door shut in alarm.

"Holy Christ!" she cried.

There was money everywhere. The floor was carpeted with wads of ten pound notes, boxes of notes on the table, money crumpled into balls of wastepaper.

"Christ he must have cracked Monte Cristo," she groaned, "There's millions here. Where did he get all this stuff?"

Sergeant Turner and Constable Crane apologized for the disturbance. Penny understood and sighed up the stairs before them.

"Such an embarrassment," she said leading them to the annex, "I should have listened to Father Tom."

Turner smiled and shrugged his shoulders.

"Father Tom had him spotted a mile away," he said.

"I'll leave you officers alone," Penny smiled said, opening the door for them.

"Thanks ma'am."

They rooted there for ten minutes and when they came downstairs, Penny had a pot of tea brewed.

"Not a thing up there," Turner sighed.

"Clean as a whistle," added Constable Crane.

"Any harm to ask what you expected to find," she asked innocently.

"A few paintings that are missing from Carrick House maybe and jewelry. He likes jewelry, just like a jackdaw."

"But nothing?"

They shook their heads and looked grimly at her.

"What did he do all day, Mrs. Wyse?" Turner pried.

"I believe he was writing a book. That's what he told me. He said a friend in Limerick was going to print it for him. But you never know, do you?"

"You never know with his type," Sergeant Turner said and Crane nodded.

They thanked her for the tea and she ushered them to the door.

Penny Wyse had no idea the money was forged or that it was a year premature. In her bedroom she threw notes in the air and laughed and rolled in the thousands and thousands of pounds. He had stolen it, she was certain, and he wouldn't be coming back for it. According to Turner, Turbo was going to gaol. It was hers now. And how she would blow it! Live life to the hilt in sunny Spain or maybe Monte Carlo. She could feel cocktails slither down her throat. At last the life of royalty. Maybe even buy a race horse. The Elms would go on the market next year and she would live the other life.

After dark, as she sat by the fire with a tumbler of gin in one hand and *Ulysses* in the other, there was an urgent knock on the door. It was Downwave and he marched past her as usual.

"What in the name of Christ happened to that shaggin' fool Tracy?" he thundered. "They have him in the clink, Penny!"

"What can I do for you, Mr. Downwave?"

"I want to collect something from his room."

"The police were here before you. Out of the goodness of my heart and in consideration for your poor wife and children, I refrained from mentioning you were an associate of his."

Gerard walked around the drawing room in circles. His eyes darted at her every now and then. If the law had the loot, that was the end of the revolution for a while. And the movement was five hundred pounds the poorer.

"How's your revolution coming along," Penny asked, as if reading his thoughts.

"You have a place in the revolution!" he shot back, flopping into a chair. "We need people like you too, you know."

Downwave told of the role the gentry had played in Irish politics since time began and Penny had a flash of how she would look in uniform, atop of a white stallion. Molly Bloom on a white stallion, riding high with two bandoliers of lead! Yes! Yes! She smiled and he sensed she was coming around. But she was thinking of the money under her bed. They spoke in double talk for an hour or so, and when Gerard was being overwhelmed by a desire to seduce her, she yawned and said, "I've had a long day Mr. Downwave, I'll see you to the door."

Penny's intuition led her to remove the money from her bedroom and that night she brought the hoard to the attic, just in case.

Father White checked on the prisoner every day or so and reported back to Penny. Turbo was like a sparrow in the cage, he said, hopping and chirping for freedom. He would get at least two years for his offences and maybe longer if more charges came to light before the court.

"I still cannot understand why he spent so long here," the priest said one evening at the Elms.

"We'll never know Father Tom. The whole affair has been a terrible strain on me, do you know what I mean?"

"I can imagine. You look drained."

"I was actually thinking of going to London for a few weeks in the New Year."

"Visiting Jill?"

"Yes. I need the break."

"By the way, a certain party told me Downwave has been coming here. You never said."

"Father Tom! Sometimes I could wring your neck! He came to see the lodger."

"I'm sorry Penny, it's just he's another bad egg."

It was raining some nights later when Downwave came to the Elms. He smiled and said he had good news for her. Tracy had smuggled a cryptic message from the Bridewell through an insider.

"Penny, he has a fortune hidden in your house!"

"What!"

She was alarmed. When he saw the terrified look on her face, Downwave laughed, a loud evil laugh. He rubbed his hands with glee and suggested places where Turbo might have hidden the stash. Penny shook her head,

"The police searched his rooms with a fine comb. There's nothing here."

"There is," he said coldly, his beady eyes strip searching her, "I know there is. Think it over Mrs. Wyse. I'll be back tomorrow."

He frightened her and she felt that chill again. She heard him laughing through the rain, a black mocking laugh. Nightmarish.

Father Tom never saw Penny so upset. Panic stricken, she arrived at the parochial house and sobbed in his arms. He stroked the back of her neck like an old lover. Why had she not come to him earlier he whispered? Was there blackmail involved? What way did Downwave threaten her? It was time to settle him, Father White said. Have him arrested and thrown into jail with Tracy. There was not going to be a revolution, he said, it was all a threat, an idle threat. Downwave wanted to make her feel insecure, a prelude to seduction. He accompanied Penny back to the Elms and stayed with her until well past midnight. She brought a shotgun to bed and had an uneasy sleep.

She never saw Gerard Downwave again. The police swooped on his house before dawn the next morning and carried him away with two sacks of propaganda and incendiary material. He was charged there and then with treason and they locked him in the Bridewell, two cells away from Turbo. Penny breathed easily and returned to *Ulysses* and Molly Bloom. In a couple of weeks she would be away to London. The sooner the better, Father Tom was leaning on her a bit. Making very subtle passes.

Downwave and Tracy were tried on the same day. There was no great interest in their plights and the courtroom was empty apart from the police and Father White. Their hearings were short and sour. Turbo got three years and Gerard got seven. There were no protests outside the courthouse when they were led to separate prison wagons, each handcuffed to two policemen. Gerard was bedraggled and bewildered; Turbo looked debonair, in cape, suit, cuff links and pocket watch. The wagons rumbled slowly out of Barnagweeha, rain falling in cascades.

For the umteenth time, Gerard Downwave asked his guards, "How many years did I get?"

They ignored his natter and wondered if what Father White had said in court was true after all, that intelligence had rotted the teacher's reason. Downwave had taught one of the guards, Tull MacHassbug, and the young man in blue stared out the rear window of the wagon to avoid his old teacher's eyes. He counted rain drops like he did during school days. Through the rain he could see the blur of Tracy's wagon trailing behind, but lost sight of it when they entered the woods of Derramore, where the oak trees blocked out light and rain with their knitted branches.

Turbo Tracy was cheerful for a man going to prison on a wet day.

"Anyone like to buy a watch?" he asked, "A good watch. Don't need it where I'm going."

His guards shook their heads.

"Cuff links?"

Again no takers.

"Alright," he said, "I'll tell ye what I'll do. May I at least show you the watch?"

They shrugged and gave him leeway to take the piece from his pocket.

"Solid gold, and paid for. Alright, I'm going to swing this watch like a pendulum. Keep yer eyes on it and when I stop, tell me how many times it swung. Closest answer gets Uncle Turbo's gold watch."

They were puzzled. But it would pass the time and shorten the road.

"Right!" Turbo quipped, looking from one to the other.

The watch dangled and slowly swayed. Their eyes followed it... one-two, three-four, five-six-seven. It built up steam and swished like a scythe within inches of their knees. Turbo summoned up all the power he had in his lifetime and the gold pocket watch hummed to and fro, pulling the guards' heads this way and that. They were magnetized to it and Turbo booted up the energy until he had their heads arced.

"Gentlemen," purred Turbo, "how is our count?"

"Twelve."

"Sixty-six."

Their voices were hollow. They looked like puppets, ghost faced they stared where the watch had been. Their eyes were cloudy.

"Way out," said Turbo. "Open the cuffs."

Keys jangled, and Tom and Jerry released Turbo and stared at the floor of the prison wagon.

He told them to stop the vehicle half way through the woods of

Derramore and after a little persuasion he turned the driver into a zombie to make three. He solicited their money and instructed them to torch the prison wagon.

"Out for the count," he muttered.

"Nineteen," muttered the driver.

Turbo faced his guards eastwards and sent them searching for the cow that jumped over the moon. They plodded in the direction of Shanahevera and the hypnotist darted through the trees to a safe house in Barr Trá.

The newspaper headlines were bold.

PRISON GUARDS TAKEN HOSTAGE

REVOLUTIONARIES GET WRONG WAGON

One paper had a one word headline that took up the width of the front page – DERRAMORE. Underneath was a photograph of the charred prison wagon with men in trench coats sifting through it.

The country was up in arms. When all seemed to be quenched in the western outback, a prison wagon is ambushed by persons unknown, believed to be aligned to Gerard Downwave, an up until now written-off nuisance. Paranoia. Desperados lurked out there in the bogs and mountains. Suddenly, Downwave became a big noise and was allotted his own team of investigators. They asked hundreds of questions about his revolution and he called them names for the first two days.

The military and the police, backed up by the reserves, were sieving through the countryside for the guards, Tracy and the rescuers. The town shook with soldiers running up and down the streets. Shops were open day and night, and Bridgey Looney ran out of porter after the second day. It was a big manhunt and the roads crawled with reporters and officials seeking information about anything from the revolution to the weather. But nobody knew anything about anything. More officers were drafted in. They set up HQ at the Elms and Penny was run off her feet, making beds, cooking meals and worrying about the money in the attic. But they were nice officers. Cavalry School. She latched on to one fellow, Captain Mountfield.

One night when Father White was returning from a game of cards with the officers, he heard snatches of a drunken song coming from Peter Egan's – "The Ambush of Derramore."

> *And when we thought the flame was quenched,*
> *And all our patriots blood spilled in vain,*
> *The bold and gallant Turbo Tracy*
> *Was freed again at Derramore.*

The priest's ulcer flared up like burning petrol and he smelled changes in the wind. Something had shifted balance. People hummed about the guerrillas, folklore was being forged. He shivered at the thought of Tracy being a hero. It was depressing. The authorities were making no headway in the case. At the parochial house he was host to a Redemptorist priest who was ever ready to intercede with the guerillas. There was not even a ransom note and Downwave was singing dumb, the officers told him. It's a mystery, they said, a total mystery.

Mountfield estimated there might be up to twelve heavily-armed fighters behind the ambush. He told Father Tom they were all locals, had to be, to vanish into the ground like they did. Every house would be searched, he whispered, every house. Father White nodded and patted him on the back.

After seven days questioning under a naked light bulb, Gerard Downwave was found dead in his cell. The newspapers were blunt:

DOWNWAVE DEAD

JAIL DEATH

BACKLASH EXPECTED

Turbo Tracy was shocked.

"Misguided poor devil," he muttered. "It killed him."

Gerard Downwave was waked at home and brought straight to the graveyard at noon the next day. His coffin was carried by four men with fair hair and blue eyes. Gretta and Irene, two of his daughters, walked behind the pallbearers, at the head of a clutch of grandchildren. Behind them, wearing dark glasses and black veil, came his wife Mabel, linked by Biddy Flanagan and The Healer Hawkins. It was the first time in twelve years anyone had seen her, they had forgotten how good-looking she was.

It was the biggest funeral ever seen in Barnagweeha and the military and police lined the streets and cordoned the town like a corral. There was not a spare soldier in town. The reporters and cameramen came from the four corners of the globe to relay the strange tension that gripped this part of the world. The funeral wound through town like a big serpent and just as silent. At the graveyard there were no prayers, no shots, no speeches. It was the quietist day that dawned for years. Still and silent until the first shovel of clay crunched on the coffin. Then Irene Downwave wailed and Pat Nixon got hysterical.

Then Penny Wyse, who insisted on going to the funeral disguised as a reporter with Captain Mountfield, suddenly broke down and was overcome with a tide of guilt. Hector Mountfield brought her head against his chest. He suggested in a whisper that they slip home and led her away, his coat wrapped around her.

Pitch pine burning, burning quickly...Mountfield smelled the fire just seconds before he turned the corner.

"Waahhuu!"

The Elms was engulfed in flames. He stood speechless at the top of the street, Penny bawling on his chest, rows of soldiers standing to attention, staring towards the graveyard. Mountfield pointed his finger and spluttered, "Fire! Fire!"

Two shots were accidently discharged and then there was a stampede to the burning manse. The roof caved in before they reached the avenue and the fire roared out of control. Huge black smuts danced and curled in the draught. Burning paper floated over roof tops like snowflakes on fire. They were falling rapidly when the mourners were returning from the funeral. In two minutes Church Street was plunged into chaos. The street screamed and leaped with people running and jumping after thousands of hovering, smoldering tenners. Shielding Penny Wyse from the debacle, Mountfield shouted at the soldiers, "Stop them! Stop them!"

The rest is history.

Time Passes
I was moved to write this story after reading a poem in Irish about our town by fellow Ennisymon writer, the late Tadhg O hÉaghráin. The title is a nod to Dylan Thomas and his play for voices, "Under Milkwood." "Time Passes" was first read on KPFA radio in Berkeley, California in 1986 and has been published several times since. The song 'Memories' by Ron Kavana is based on this story.

For the Record
This is the first story that I published. I wrote it after a long party of music and storytelling in Galway. It first appeared in *Criterion 83*, a Galway literary magazine.

Limbo
Snapshot of my school days. It is included in *Modern Fiction about School Teaching: An Anthology.*

Bláth na Spéire
This was written while I was collecting tunes and stories from the last tradition bearers in Doolin, County Clare.

Revolution
No idea how this came to me. Long nights in bad company, maybe.

The Warrior Carty
The spoken word version of this is popular with listeners of Clare FM. This story is included in *The Clare Anthology.*

Derramore
Turbo Tracy, the main character in "Derramore," just popped into my head one day and the story wrote itself. I was living in Oakland, California at the time and knocking around with an Irish band called The Mild Colonial Boys.

Audio Edition
To receive an audio edition of *The West*, email the ISBN # of this book to info@tintaun.com.

Eddie Stack was born in County Clare, in the west of Ireland. His short fiction has appeared in several anthologies, magazines and literary journals. He also wrote *Out of the Blue,* a collection of stories, and *Heads,* a novel set in San Francisco.

www.eddiestack.com

ACKNOWLEDGEMENTS

Thanks to John Fitzpatrick, Tom Liddy, Ollie Liddy, Bill O'Brien, Matt O'Dea, John Norton, Phillip Morrison, Alan Wherry, Ellen Murphy and Marie O'Sullivan for helping to get this edition published.

Thanks to the late Danny Cassidy for his friendship and support.

Very special thanks to Kathleen Sullivan.

Lightning Source UK Ltd.
Milton Keynes UK
UKHW042231280619
345236UK00001B/23/P